SEBASTIAN SHEPHERD

and the Mystery of the Dead Water

To the Downums,

God Bless

Jamey A. Gilliland

Jas. 3:13

SEBASTIAN SHEPHERD

and the Mystery of the Dead Water

JAMEY A. GILLILAND

TATE PUBLISHING & Enterprises

Published by Tate Publishing & Enterprises, LLC
127 E. Trade Center Terrace | Mustang, Oklahoma 73064 USA
1.888.361.9473 | www.tatepublishing.com

Tate Publishing is committed to excellence in the publishing industry. The company reflects the philosophy established by the founders, based on Psalms 68:11,

"The Lord gave the word and great was the company of those who published it."

Book design copyright © 2007 by Tate Publishing, LLC. All rights reserved.

Illustrations by Evan R. Clark
Cover design by Eddie Russell
Interior design by Janae J. Glass

Published in the United States of America

ISBN: 978-1-60462-130-3
1. Juvenile Fiction: Ages 10-15   2. Action
3. Adventure   4. Fantasy

07.10.12

This book is dedicated to my one true love.
Sandy, without you, none of this is possible.
I love you.

THANKS

There are so many people to thank regarding the writing and production of this book. This is not an exhaustive list, so please forgive me if I leave someone out. First and foremost, I want to thank my Lord and Savior Jesus Christ. You are the great king under the mountain who graciously directs our paths. Next, I want to thank my beautiful wife, Sandy, who has been an ever constant support in this project. Your words of wisdom and encouragement have been invaluable to me. Thanks to Mom and Dad, Susan, Kim, Henry, Haley, and William. I also want to thank the rest of the Gilliland, McAllister, and Larimore families for your kindness and support.

The following people have had a significant impact on the development of the book. Evan Clark for the illustrations. Sarah Richards for the first cover art used in the original submission. Adam and Keitra Beach for prayer support and encouragement. Lester Orwig for his Hebrew transliterations. Blair Rogers and the Rogers family for their insight into first draft of the book. Debbie Lipscomb and Chris Fuller for their edit and helpful critiques. The staff of Tate Publishing for your professionalism and talent in making this dream become a reality. To Page and Ashley Brooks for your encouragement. To the good people of New Orleans Baptist Theological Seminary, Rogers Baptist Association, North Park Trinity Baptist Church, and the Christian community at large that has been a source of prayer and encouragement.

A special thanks and encouragement goes out to all students at Rogers State University, especially those involved with BCM and FCA. You have all been very supportive and understanding and a frequent source of inspiration. Also, thanks to Baptist College Ministers all over the country, every student I've ever ministered with and every partner in ministry I've had the pleasure of serving. I hope this book encourages you as well. Finally, I would like to thank you, the reader. I hope this book is useful and entertaining. May God richly bless you, and I hope to meet you some day.

Blessings to you,
Jamey A. Gilliland

CHARACTERS

Mai: The great king under the mountain. One who established the order of the Elders.

Sebastian Corvin: Son of Cakal Corvin and ward of Jeanine the Elder

Jeanine the Elder: The only Elder left in Crespin after the great Exodus.

Bolo Brooks: Friend to Sebastian, is unsure of himself.

Shawndra Baker: Friend to Sebastian, wishes to be a soldier.

Cakal Corvin: Father to Sebastian, former captain of the Citadel, mysteriously disappeared after he went to find his brother, Nabal Corvin.

Nabal Corvin: Disappeared after leaving for Sodorrah with Aswan.

Gilroy the Elder: One of the first Elders, believed to have gone into the eternity.

Rowland: Former apprentice to Jeroboam, leader of the Elders. Now pledged to Jeanine.

Jeroboam: Leader of the Elders that led them into the great exodus.

Ivveleth: The name for the nine judges who rule over judicial matters in Crespin.

Halal Ba'ar: Member of the Ivveleth, father of Ba'ar, and most vocal critic of the Elders.

Ba'ar Ba'ar: Son of Halal and most accomplished soldier at the Citadel.

William Hart: Captain of the Citadel due to the absence of Cakal Corvin.

Pithe: A simple-minded member of the Ivveleth, the pawn of Halal.

Balam: Sebastian's spirited horse

Baruk: Large wolf-like beasts that live in the granite mountains. Can sense truth and deception. Powerful and stealthy.

Skiatook: Son of the head of the Baruk Clan, Kronos.

Verdigris: Son of Kronos with green eyes and grey fur.

Kronos: Aged leader of all Baruk, father of Skiatook and Verdigris, and blood brother to Cakal Corvin.

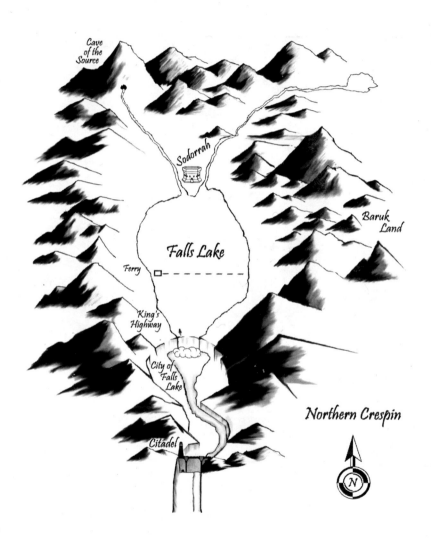

1NTRODUCTION

Before men were sons of prosperity and women were daughters of virtue, there was a time of great confusion and loss. This was a time when the king had been exiled and the soldiers of the great fortress called the Citadel were more skilled at herding sheep than protecting cities. The land of Crespin had gone too long without the deeds of heroes or the wisdom of the Elders. It was the time of the dead water.

The truth of the harshness of this time has been replaced by fanciful fables that please the senses and tickle the ears. Storytellers leave out the great furnace of hardships and the uncertainty that forged the iron of men's resolve. They leave out the fact that almost all civilization had been lost and Crespin was but a hairsbreadth away from falling into darkness for eternity.

I am the last of the Elders, and I was present when

these things came to pass. For this reason, I have recorded the history of Crespin. Our truth must be known so that our people may learn from our past. May you, the reader, learn of our trials and triumphs and be encouraged that in your dark hour you may look to the light and see that a hero is waiting to be summoned. May you know that our greatest king was once a small shepherd boy, our greatest queen was once a slave, and our greatest heroes were once unsure wanderers in the dark. Now, read on, and learn about the history of Sebastian the shepherd and the mystery of the dead water.

DEATH OF A CITY

The morning was cold and damp in Falls Lake as Lady Jeanine briskly walked along the pathway that led to the house of Cakal Corvin. Her robes flapped in the wind behind her as she ducked around corners and took the shortest route to her destination. Time was not her friend, and she had to steal seconds where she could.

Just four days ago she had traveled to the Valley of Dry Bones to say farewell to Gilroy the Elder, the great leader that had been her mentor. He was one of the first Elders in Crespin so many ages ago. When the first King of Crespin was crowned, he was there. When the foundations of the great city of Falls Lake were laid, he was there. He himself led the ovation when Jeanine was given her Elder's robe after she had journeyed to the source of the spring and faced Mai. Jeanine could hardly believe it when

Gilroy had told her that the whisperings of Mai were on the wind and in his ear telling him that his final journey was drawing near. She traveled with the Elder to the mouth of the valley where he steadied himself and then marched into the deep dark chasm in the earth, leaving Lady Jeanine standing alone clutching the book of Armagh that he had left in her keeping.

Lady Jeanine's tearful goodbye with her old friend was interrupted when a messenger from the Citadel found her. This red-faced boy about sixteen years old, panted so hard that once he finally reached Jeanine, he couldn't speak. She was still looking intently into the dark abyss of the valley where her mentor had passed into eternity, as the boy, still gasping for breath and struggling to stay on his feet, staggered up beside her. Jeanine knew the boy as Rowland, the apprentice to Jeroboam, the new leader of the Elders. She thought Rowland was a good-natured boy but a little too simple minded. To be an Elder, one must be aware of evil, as well as good. An Elder had to learn to be shrewd and as crafty as a serpent while being as wise as an old wood owl. Rowland, however, knew more about farming and fishing than being an Elder. Still, she admired his sincerity as well as his ability to occasionally make her laugh. The lady stood patiently waiting for the moment of exhaustion to pass while the boy, bent at the waist and clutching his chest and side, struggled to stay on his feet.

Lady Jeanine took a water skin from under her robe and said, "Drink this, it will help." Rowland put the silver spout to his lips and tipped up the skin and took a deep gulp and instantly knew that he was drinking living water from the Falls. The sweet taste of the water was soothing to his parched mouth and dry throat. His shortness of breath quickly faded, and he had renewed energy in his arms and legs. He was able to stand up straight immediately and faced the Elder with surprise.

"I didn't know you could keep the water alive in a skin," said Rowland as if he had just learned a deep secret.

"You can't," said Jeanine as she took the water skin, put the cap back on it, and stored it out of sight beneath her cloak. "But I can." Her cloak and traveling robes were embroidered with stitching that made it appear as if a single vine curled about her. The vine wound its way down the front collar and around the bottom, as well as the ends of her sleeves. This was the common dress of all the Elders. The symbol of Crespin was the fruitful vine. With the living water flowing through the Jezreel River, it seemed a fitting symbol. "Now, you didn't come all this way just for the challenge. It's a long way from here to Falls Lake. Why don't you tell me your message?"

"Forgive me, my lady," said Rowland as he bowed low. "I was sent to tell you that Cakal's wife is laboring in difficulty with her child and is due to give birth any day. Your presence is requested to bless the child, and if need be, save their lives."

"I thought she was in Falls Lake. How could she be having difficulty with her labor unless…" Lady Jeanine looked past Rowland and seemed as if she were sifting through all the parchments in her mind that she had read throughout the countless years of her life. The sorrow of saying goodbye to her friend Gilroy had left her, and the concern over this news was becoming more intense.

As she traveled back through her mind, she heard the whispers of Elders that had long since passed from Crespin. They were all speaking now, and Jeanine's mind began to spin. Their language was warning her of ominous change. There was excitement and dread for the days ahead. The noise would have overcome a normal person and might have even driven them mad, but then again, a simpleton would not have heard them. The voices began to hush as a vision of the sun setting behind a mountain overcame her consciousness.

In her vision, she journeyed into a cave where a great rock with intricate carvings could be seen. The rock was weeping. From a crack down the center of the tall granite wall in the back of the cave came shining tears of joy. From another crack came a black sludge that was made up of tears of betrayal. These tears flowed down and intermingled into a black oil that ran down the face of the rock, onto the ground and spread out over everything. The dark water turned into a flood and raged out, poisoning and killing all that it touched. Jeanine was breathing shallowly, and her mouth was open. She would turn away, but she was powerless to move and powerless to stop it. And then she saw a child. A baby lying in the path of the dead water. But when the water seemed as if it would wash the infant away, it stopped and drew back. It was as if the dark oily liquid feared the child. And then she awoke.

Lady Jeanine felt as though she had just run a marathon with Rowland. She was drained and weary in her soul and struggled to keep from collapsing to the ground. The vision was exhausting. She reached in her cloak and recovered the flask with the living water and drank deeply. The water refreshed her and crystallized her thinking once again. Now, freshly awake and out of her daze, she managed to whisper to Rowland, "Why do the other Elders require my presence with Cakal's wife?"

"That's just it," said Rowland. "They and their apprentices started packing their rucksacks and getting ready to leave Falls Lake in an awful hurry. I've never seen anything like it." Rowland scratched his head of thin brown hair. All these things were beyond an apprentice that had only been following his master for ten years. "One of the things that confuses me the most is that we never travel together in large groups 'cause it's too dangerous. But this time, all of them are going to the same place. And do you know where that is?" said Rowland as if he were going to give Jeanine some surprising information.

"They're coming here," said Lady Jeanine.

"They're coming he...Yeah! How did you know?"

"We must not be here when they arrive. If we are to speak with them we must do so on the road between here and Falls Lake." Jeanine turned, looked at Rowland, and said, "I'm sorry to ask this of you, but we must leave this place quickly and get back to Falls Lake. Can you make this journey again?"

"I can do whatever you ask," said Rowland. He wasn't much for complaining. "I may need a few more sips from your water skin if we have to keep the same pace, but I'll make do."

It took a traveler three days to journey from Falls Lake to the Valley of Dry Bones on foot. Jeanine and Rowland made it in one. Something troubled Lady Jeanine that she could not explain. Deep in her soul a worried spirit warned her of danger. Her experience at the valley where she heard the voices and saw the vision left her startled and bewildered. The vision and the voices were for her benefit. All Elders were taught to trust their instincts that they have been given by the Great Mai. If there was unrest in Jeanine's soul, then there was unrest in the land.

Mai was the maker of all Crespin and the great king under the mountain. He was not a man, but he took great interest in the deeds of men. Mai appointed the first man king to rule according to his will. Mai also called the first twelve Elders to his service. Every apprentice who wished to be an Elder was required to face Mai in the cave of the well spring as their final trial. If an apprentice succeeded, he would drink from the pure spring and receive power to be Mai's servant and an Elder. If he failed and still drank from the spring, the consequences were terrible.

Jeanine hurried to Falls Lake with a heavy heart. She had met all of the Elders as they were on their way to the valley from which she had just come. They told her that Cakal Corvin, Captain of the Guard of the Citadel and most loyal servant of the King of Crespin, had left more than seven days ago to find his lost brother Nabal. Cakal's younger brother, Nabal, was a foolish man. Nabal had left more than four weeks before with Lady Jeanine's apprentice to journey upriver, beyond the Falls, to Sodorrah. Jeanine's apprentice was the young and beautiful Aswan. She was fair to look upon, tall and willowy, and wise beyond her years. She was by far one of Lady Jeanine's greatest apprentices. Her eyes showed her compassion, and her voice reflected her strength. Nabal fancied Aswan, but her life was dedicated to the training of an Elder. On her thirty-second birthday, Aswan set out on her journey as was the appropriate age for an apprentice to face the final trial of becoming an Elder. Nabal was to travel with her upriver as far as the fishing village of Sodorrah. There Nabal and Aswan were to part ways.

Aswan would go on alone to the cave, and Nabal would go about his business in Sodorrah. The entire journey should not have taken over ten days. However, it had been more than thirty days, and Aswan had not returned. Also, no one knew where Nabal was.

All these things swarmed in the mind of Jeanine as she rushed to Falls Lake to be with Cakal's wife. His wife was having a difficult labor, and the message for her to return was over three days old. The Elder and the ragged looking Rowland had not slept or eaten since they left from the valley in the hope of returning soon enough to be of some help. Her hope was fading with the sunlight.

Now, as Jeanine made her way through the winding stone pathways of the great city of Falls Lake, she couldn't help but notice that there was an uncomfortable silence in the air. Jeanine thought to herself, *There should be laughing.* She had parted from Rowland and told him not to stop to eat or sleep because she was unsure of how safe Falls Lake was for them. Jeanine told Rowland, "Go to the storage room in the hall of the Elders and fill two rucksacks with all the food they will hold. Also, take my silver flask and fill it with water from the fountain in the courtyard of the Elders. Then go to the small house beside the Citadel and wait for me there." Off he went into the long shadows of the evening as Jeanine couldn't shake the feeling that time for her and the city was running short.

The birth of a child was a joyous occasion in a

land that was plentiful. It was a time for the mother to be pampered and for fathers to laugh loudly and to boast about all that their children will become. Families were to tell jokes and be comforting and not a hindrance. It was a time for baby talk and grand dreams for a new life. Falls Lake was a proper city for such a scene. The city was enchanting and alive with energy. The great waterfall that cascaded over the edge of a granite cliff was the very heart of the city. The churning mist was saturated with life that flowed from deep within the mountains where the Great Mai dwelled.

Most expectant mothers journeyed to Falls Lake the month before their child was due in order to be strengthened by the life-giving mists. If the life of Cakal's wife was indeed in danger, this was a bad omen. Whatever was wrong with her, the living water of the falls could not make right. Lady Jeanine had to hurry.

Elders were always in haste but never in a hurry. To see an Elder tussled as if they had just walked through the whistling caves or winded as if they had just run a marathon to Crescent City and back was a bad omen. This meant that serious consequences were about to take place. Elders arrived in their own time and in their own fashion. They asked no one's leave and were present where needed, regardless of whether their presence was convenient or wanted. Jeanine's hair was mussed and blown, and her garments were dirty and stained. She had no time for pride or appearance and only thought of making her way to Cakal's home.

Jeanine walked through the city in the way of the Elders. She was making a rhythmic tap, tap, tapping noise on the pavement stones with her ironwood staff as she walked. She would tap the third stone from the edge two times, the ornate stone in the middle once and the next three stones in quick succession. There were definite patterns that the Elders used in different parts of the city. They rehearsed the patterns wherever they walked, but they always seemed to use them in Falls Lake.

The city itself seemed to step aside for the hurried lady. It seemed as if alleys changed and pillars moved to accommodate the needs of the Elders. In Falls Lake people said that the walls were alive, along with the water. Children would make a game of seeing how long they could follow an Elder before they disappeared. A group of children would follow one of the aged Elders, listening to their rhythmic tapping noise on the stones and then as soon as they turned a corner the children would rush ahead as fast as they could only to find a blocked alley and no Elder. No one but the Elders knew the secret of this, but it didn't stop people from making up their own stories.

Jeanine saw the house of Cakal Corvin that was built on the west side of the falls, as were many houses like it. They were all stacked against each other as if they were soldiers awaiting inspection. The tan stones were chiseled from a quarry outside of the canyon. Friends of the family of the Corvins had journeyed from the Agriplaines to tend to the expectant mother and dutiful husband, but they were all standing outside of the house in small huddles speaking in hushed reverence. Once again, Jeanine said to herself, *There should be laughing.*

There should definitely have been laughing. But this gathering of people looked as if they were attending a funeral instead of a birth. She did not see the Captain of the Guard, to whom the house belonged. *Has Captain Corvin not returned yet?* she asked herself, yet feared the answer.

"Move aside, I must not be hindered," said Jeanine to two members of the House of Ivveleth who were standing in the narrow path, along with a small boy that looked as if he had rather be anywhere else but there.

"Of course," said the taller of the two men. "We must not inconvenience an Elder," he said with a tone of sarcasm. The other man started to move out of Jeanine's way but ceased with a stern look from the tall man. The tall man's name was Halal Ba'ar. Halal was the most vocal critic of the Elders in the Ivveleth. Both men were dressed in their formal robes that identified their office. The House of Ivveleth consisted of nine judges appointed by the king from among the people to settle arguments regarding the law. In the event that the king of Crespin could not fulfill his duties, the judges would rule in his absence.

The traditional robes of the Ivveleth were solid black. That was all that was required, but the Ivveleth sought to be highly fashionable and did as much with the color black as one could imagine. Their long robes reached to the ground and made a swishing sound as they walked. The local people called them street sweepers behind their backs. Their large sleeves looked as if they could smuggle a Baruk cub past the guards without being noticed. Their collars were high and made of black velvet that ended in a black leather strip on the front where black shell buttons fastened the robe. Lady Jeanine had no time or respect for such self-important fashion. Elders were not given to pomp and circumstance and were known to be of ill temper with those who were.

The other man with Halal was Pithe, also dressed in Ivveleth robes. Pithe was not convincingly bright and generally did what Halal told him. It was clear to most that he was appointed to the Ivveleth for that purpose. The Ivveleth were to be stewards of the law in all regions of Crespin. However, following Halal's questionable appointment, more and more decisions handed down by the House of Ivveleth seemed to pay no regard to justice but gave more power to themselves. The Elders had begun questioning and speaking out against the rulings and, as a result, caused much conflict between the two groups—particularly between Halal and Lady Jeanine. Jeanine saw dark aspirations behind Halal's eyes, and she did not trust him. No, she did not trust him at all.

"I don't have time to banter with you, Halal," said Jeanine in a huff.

"Now don't be rude, I only wanted to introduce my son to you. I don't believe the two of you have met." The four-year-old son of Halal Ba'ar was tall for his age and had a lean look about him. "I've been considering enrolling him in the Citadel guard when he is old enough. He can learn to use a sword."

Jeanine looked at the boy and then to his father and said, "Crespin would be better served if their children were taught how to use their minds first. Nevertheless, I have heard you had a son, but I have not heard his name."

"His name is Ba'ar," said Halal as he pulled Ba'ar's arm roughly so that the boy stood in front of Lady Jeanine. Ba'ar winced in pain and tried to work his arm free from his father's grip, but with a rough nudge and menacing look from Halal, the boy realized his struggling was pointless. The four-year-old stood straight, trying to hide the gnawing fear he had of this woman standing before him. "Remember this day, Ba'ar," said Halal. "A day will come when there won't be any Elders left in the land and you will be able to tell everyone that you met the last one face to face in the great city." Halal smiled wickedly. Ba'ar looked at his father and then tried to mimic the same menacing smile.

"I'll be around long enough to see the end of

corruption among the Ivveleth. And if you think that you can advance whatever sinister plans are bouncing around in that hollow head of yours just because the family of Cakal Corvin is distracted, you are mistaken. We still have a king," said Jeanine as she pointed a bony finger at Halal.

"Oh, I'd say that Corvin is more than distracted. I'd be surprised if he ever recovers, that is, if he returns. And as for the king, we shall see." Halal laughed as he turned and took his son in tow. It was as if he were dragging a small cart behind him. The two men and the boy turned the corner, and Halal's laughter faded into the mists.

Lady Jeanine was alarmed by Halal's comments and resumed her path to Cakal's house. As the Elder approached the house she was seen by those standing outside. They stepped away from the house's entrance, and she passed by them without a side glance. *Maybe I should have renewed my body in order to get here faster,* she thought to herself. *Then I would know what was going on. No, we Elders must not waste our energy and power on vanity or impatience. All is in the hands of Mai.* As the lady began to step into the house, she met William Hart, second in command of the Citadel and closest friend to Captain Corvin.

"William, what in Crespin is going on here? All these dawdlers about have set me in a bad temper. And you look as though you have a dark cloud hanging over you as well. Quickly, tell me the news," ordered Lady Jeanine.

"Captain Corvin's wife has died," said Hart. The words stung the Elder's ears as she braced herself to hear the rest of the news. William continued, "She died just before dawn this morning." William's head hung low as if a great weight rested on his neck. He stood outside of the house wearing the polished armor of a knight of the Citadel. The bright shine on the metal seemed to mock his dull spirit. Lady Jeanine noticed the gold medallion with an engraving of the Citadel that hung around his neck.

"Why are you wearing Cakal's medallion of rank? That is the Captain's medallion, and it should not be worn unless the Captain has resigned his rank, or he is dead," said Jeanine as her eyes narrowed, realizing that though the news of Corvin's wife's death was terrible, she might not have heard the worst of it.

"Captain Corvin placed it on me and appointed me the Captain while he is away," said Hart. "I am to deliver you the message that he has gone to find his lost brother and bring him back home. However, the Captain has not returned and surely does not know of the loss of his wife. I don't know how I will tell him that he has lost his wife, and maybe his brother, in the same season." Hart did not look Jeanine in the eye but kept looking toward the ground.

"What about his child?" asked Jeanine in a frantic, nearly panicked voice. "Is the child well? Was the birth successful?" There was desperation in her words.

"The child is well. A local woman is keeping him. She has seen to his care." Hart straightened his shoulders and once again looked like a strong soldier as he turned and began walking back toward the Citadel. He stopped and turned to Lady Jeanine and said, "The Captain's wishes and his wife's last request were that you should watch over their only child until he returns. You are the only one the Captain will trust with the life of his child. The Ivveleth have already tried to come and claim the home, but I bore witness to your stewardship of all that is the Captain's. Now, if you will excuse me, I have delivered my Captain's message. These are the wishes of Cakal Corvin the brave. I will be at the Citadel if you need me." Hart turned back to the path that would take him to the entrance to Falls Lake and the Citadel. His armor would glisten in the sunlight had there been any breaking through the thick mists. The sun was setting, and it seemed as though all of nature joined Jeanine in her sorrow for Cakal's wife and her frustration at Cakal himself. She was frustrated that a man would leave his wife at such a difficult time. She was frustrated that the Elders had left in such a mysterious fashion and had chosen her to stay behind alone and bear witness to such ill tidings. She was frustrated that she didn't know more about how all these events were related.

"This is outrageous!" Jeanine muttered to herself. She whirled around quickly and called out to Hart as he was walking away. "Well, are you going to tell me the child's name or does Cakal the brave wish to leave that to me as well?"

Hart turned and called back in a loud voice so as not to be drowned out by the nearby falls, "The boy's name is Sebastian, and I will do what I can to help you look after him. I am not only a servant of Crespin but also Cakal's friend." Hart turned back to his path and soon disappeared in the waning light.

Jeanine huffed and thought to herself, *Why is it always Cakal the brave or Cedric the conqueror? Why are the acclaims of men so closely linked with warfare and mutilating and ending life? Why can't they glorify the virtues of timeliness? Now, there would be a great leader. All hail Anthony the punctual. Or maybe even Vincent the efficient. But no, Ivan the terrible would be more feared. What is so desirable about being feared anyway?* Jeanine whirled about again and entered the house with such a determined look in her eyes that some of the ladies attending the baby gasped at how quickly she approached. All of her swirling thoughts and frustrations faded as soon as her eyes caught sight of the perfect little child that she would call Sebastian. "Here now, let me see him." Lady Jeanine cradled the infant in her arms and looked into his deep blue eyes. "No, you won't be Sebastian the terrible or Sebastian the destroyer if I have anything to do with it. You will be the wise or the kind or even the punctual. You will be known for saving life I think, rather than taking it. "Don't you worry, young one, I'll take care of you. But when your father returns from beyond the falls, I will give him a knocking.

A young woman came across the room and touched Lady Jeanine on the shoulder. The young lady was pregnant and soon to give birth herself. "My lady, excuse me, but I just want you to know that if my husband and I can be of any help to you, we would be glad to. You see, my husband is a baker, and I'm soon to have a baby too. If it's a boy, we will name him Sean. If it's a girl, we will name her Shawndra." The young woman smiled with warmth as she cradled her belly.

"Thank you, dear," said Lady Jeanine. "But the trip upriver to Sodorrah where Cakal's brother went only takes a few days. With much grace, they will both be back soon." Then Jeanine looked down at Cakal's son. "Don't you worry, Sebastian," she whispered. "Your father will be home soon." Jeanine then reached out and placed her palm flat on the belly of the young mother to be. Lady Jeanine smiled and said, "Shawndra is a very pretty name, very pretty indeed."

As Lady Jeanine left the Corvin house with Sebastian, wrapped in cloth and warm linen. The darkness of night began to settle in on the city of Falls Lake. The darkness brought a great unsettling in Jeanine's soul. The birds in the air were flying away from the falls, out of formation and hurriedly. She quickened her pace as she looked behind her and was thankful to see that the young woman she had just spoken with was being placed on a horse and led back out of the city. She turned away, just missing the sight of the birds falling out of the air as if they had run out of breath. Then Jeanine turned in surprise as from the direction of the falls she heard something that had never been heard in Falls Lake before. But it was unmistakable. Screams.

More and more screams could be heard from the city as something was overtaking everything. Jeanine did not know what to make of it all. Then she could hear something else. Once again, from deep within her soul, as if all the Elders from the past caught her ear and gasped out to her in one clear desperate whisper, "Run!"

Lady Jeanine didn't hesitate. She turned toward the Citadel, held little Sebastian close and ran. In other circumstances, it would be almost entertaining to see an ancient woman running past others on foot and horseback. But the Elder passed them as if they were standing still. Her cloak flew up behind her and flapped in the wind as she darted between individuals and under horses. Something was happening that was changing all of Crespin. Falls Lake was changing. Falls Lake was dying. And anyone caught inside the great city just might die with it.

A NEW BEGINNING

(13 years later)

Crespin changed. The living water ceased to flow from the mountain, and the oily stench of the dead water took its place and poisoned all that it touched. Captain Cakal Corvin never returned, and no word ever came from him or his brother in all the thirteen years of their absence. All assumed they were lost for all time. All but one of the Elders left Crespin, and no one knew where the others went or if they would ever return. The King of Crespin was exiled by the Ivveleth, which left no one to stand between their great appetite for power and the people. The Ivveleth ruled from Crescent City where they met in the hall called Halalah. Falls Lake was nearly deserted. Soldiers still lived in the Citadel, but their role changed from protector of a city to keepers of a ghost town. William

Hart became the guardian of the Citadel after Captain Corvin left. He faithfully went about the duties of a Captain, but given the condition of the city, his position was of little consequence. In the shadow of the Citadel, in a small home just big enough for two, the last citizens of Falls Lake resided. Far enough away from the falls not to be affected by the poison mists, a young boy named Sebastian was raised by Jeanine the Elder and tended sheep in the Agriplaines.

———

Sebastian carved intently on his ironwood staff which his guardian, the Elder Jeanine, had given him. She had taught him to record his own story in this way. When an Elder had a great accomplishment, he would carve the story on his staff. At the end of their days, before an Elder would pass into eternity, he would leave his staff behind so that his story would not fade away.

Two weeks ago, Sebastian had fought off a couple of snarling, foaming dogs that had been crazed by drinking from the Jezreel River, which was poisoned by the dead water. He was able to drive them both off without any of the sheep getting hurt or being bitten himself. For a thirteen-year-old boy, this was a great accomplishment. Sebastian had seen the dogs running across the hills, headed toward the flock of sheep. They were barking and snapping at small trees and each other. He thought he had seen one bite a rock as it ran past. The dead water drove any beast mad, unless it killed it first. Sebastian didn't have time to move the flock, so he stood in the space between his defenseless sheep and the ravenous dogs. He hid behind a nearby outcropping of rock. He picked up two stones, and as soon as the insane dogs were in view he hurled them toward his would-be attackers. The rocks hit each of them square on the forehead and they ran off shrieking in pain. Sebastian was excited that he had chased off the threat to the herd. He turned back toward the sheep and walked with a swagger in his step thinking, *And that is how it is done.*

His moment of victory was cut short when he heard a noise that made his blood run cold in his veins. The sounds of growling came from close behind him. Very close behind him. Sebastian whirled around just in time to avoid the snapping jaws of the dogs that had come back to continue the fight. Sebastian had no time to pick up rocks, besides, that would make him kneel down and take his eyes off of the crazed beasts. He knew that he wouldn't be able to fight them off for long with just his staff.

As the dogs squatted and coiled like springs to launch at Sebastian, a wild looking thing jumped from behind the very rocks that Sebastian had hidden behind and attacked one of the dogs. Sebastian thought that it looked like a man, but because of the shrieks and whoops that came from the hairy creature as it attacked the dogs, he wasn't quite ready to call it human. He didn't know who he wanted to win this fight. Sebastian knew how to fight wild dogs, but this thing was all together new. The dog winced in pain, wiggled free, and ran into the distance dragging one lame leg behind it. The manlike creature then turned on the other wild dog. The dog attacked him, knocking them both behind the rocks and out of Sebastian's view. The next thing he heard was a yelp of pain and a wet snapping noise and then nothing. Sebastian wanted to walk around to the other side of the rock to investigate, but his body refused to move, so Sebastian stood his ground. He would meet the winner of this combat in a moment.

The wild looking figure half walked half crawled out from behind the rocks and said, "Those nasty things won't be botherin' anyone again."

It's definitely a man, Sebastian thought. "You have saved me, for that I thank you," said Sebastian. "My name is..." he didn't get to finish his sentence when the dirty, wild-eyed man spoke.

"Your name is Sebastian, and you must live." The man had a gleam in his eyes that showed there was more to him than his dirty animal skins and matted hair. "Grow wise boy, grow strong. Your time is coming." At those words, the dirty man stepped back behind the rocks. Sebastian moved quickly with his staff in hand to question him, but found only a wild dog with a broken neck. The words of the man lingered with him, like an omen of things to come, whether good or bad.

Sebastian wanted to remember that day, even

though Lady Jeanine instructed him to tell no one of the wild man's help. Sebastian sat on the ground at the entrance to the makeshift sheep pen and intently carved the image of a dog.

The sheep pen was of crude construction. Sebastian took rocks and poles and made two walls that joined to the bottom of a cliff. They came together like a triangle, and Sebastian put the sheep inside of it. He then sat at the entrance and made sure the sheep stayed together while he worked on his staff. He became so intent on finishing carving the image on his staff that he didn't notice that a couple of the smaller sheep had gotten between a couple of loose poles, freed themselves, and were making their way to the river where the dead water flowed.

Sebastian felt a sticky warm sensation on the back of his neck, as if one of the giant leeches that were rumored to live in the mountain streams were crawling on him. Sebastian jerked around quickly to see what was upon him.

"*Agh!* You stupid horse, stop licking my neck!" cried Sebastian as he clumsily made his way to his feet. Balam was a two-year-old colt. He was a common paint horse that was uncommonly smart. Sebastian had heard a story about a talking mule whose name was Balam from Lady Jeanine, so Sebastian thought it was fitting that he name this horse the same. Besides, Balam always seemed to have something to say, if only Sebastian knew how to listen. Sebastian helped Farmer Levert with the birth of the animal. Balam's mother didn't survive the ordeal, so Sebastian fed Balam from a bottle until he was strong enough to eat on his own. Since then, Balam followed him wherever he went, even when he was not supposed to. Sebastian figured that the horse had kicked his stall door open again and run out of the barn to find his companion.

It was at that time that he heard the braying of Mr. Levert's sheep in the distance that he was paid to watch, and Sebastian knew he had little time to get to the sheep before they reached the river. "Come on, old friend, take me to the sheep, so we can keep them from getting sick in the river and keep me from getting in trouble."

The sheep were headed for the Jezreel River. They were dumb animals that didn't know well enough not to drink from the dead water. If they made it to the river's edge, they would drink and then certainly get sick and possibly die. Every farmer on the Agriplaines had lost animals at some time to the poisoned waters. When people traveled through the country, they kept their distance because if a person fell in they would become very ill. If they swallowed any of the water by accident then they would fall into a deep darkness and go mad.

It wasn't always this way. The older people in Crespin could remember a time when the water was full of life and nourished the land. When people got sore from a hard day's work, all they had to do was swim in the river and their aches would go away.

When goats and cows drank from the river, they gave more milk. And Falls Lake was a place of life and joy because the mist from the enormous falls filled the air. Now it was a deserted city where no one dared to venture.

"Mr. Levert will skin me if I let his sheep get sick," said Sebastian as he grabbed a handful of the horse's mane and swung himself onto his back. Sebastian didn't need a saddle with this horse. The young horse and rider had many adventures, and misadventures, together and were comfortable and familiar enough to anticipate each other's moves. The horse took off with a jolt, racing for the river's edge. Fortunately, the rest of the flock was still resting in the crude pen Sebastian had made, far away from the river's edge.

In his mind, Sebastian could see Farmer Levert standing with both arms crossed in front of his chest. When Levert was angry, his whole face, including his ears would turn as red as a ripe tomato. His black and gray hair seemed to stand on end, and he had a large vein on his forehead that would become very obvious. Sebastian knew this look all too well. After all, he became a shepherd three years ago in order to pay off a debt of three newly planted hills of fluxom seed when he decided to help Farmer Levert by watering them. But he used water from the river instead of water from the well. The dead water from the river killed the seeds, poisoned the dirt, and nothing could grow there until they loaded all the dirt on carts and dumped it in the river and then went and got fresh soil to put in its place. All that work and damage had long been paid off, but Sebastian found that he liked the peace and quiet of the Agriplaines better than the constant clanging and drilling of soldiers that he heard growing up next to the Citadel.

The horse and his rider raced to the sheep and stopped between them and the water. Sebastian got off the horse and with a few loud hoots and foot stomps, turned the sheep away and back toward the rest of the flock. Sebastian turned to Balam and put his hands on the horse's nose, "I apologize to you, old boy, for yelling at you when you licked my neck. If you hadn't, then I would not have noticed the sheep that got out, and they would have fallen in the water and that would be that." Sebastian petted the neck of the horse and reached into his rucksack and pulled out a green apple. "Here, old friend, consider this both my apology and your reward." Sebastian figured that it was the green apples in the summer and the dried berries in the winter that kept the horse around. However, there were times when he thought he saw glimpses of understanding in the horse's eyes.

"You had better be glad that horse got your attention. I don't think you would have made it in time," came a girl's voice from behind Sebastian. Sebastian whirled around in surprise, not knowing that anyone was in the area.

"Oh hello, Shawndra," said Sebastian. Sebastian was a little embarrassed that someone had seen his near disaster. He rubbed his head and looked at her, "So you saw all of that, did you?"

"Yes, and I was on my way down from my parent's house to deliver food to the Citadel when I saw you carving on your stick while Mr. Levert's sheep headed for the river," Shawndra said in a defiant tone with her fists propped firmly on her hips.

"It isn't just a stick, it's an ironwood staff," said Sebastian. He would have pounced on anything to divert attention away from his mistake.

"Well, it's a very nice stick," said Shawndra. "Still, you came very close to getting in serious trouble."

Shawndra was the same age as Sebastian. Both of them were thirteen years old and had known each other their whole lives. Shawndra was very intense and always seemed to have great purpose in everything she did and did not do. When Lady Jeanine would have to leave for a couple of days, she would always take Sebastian to Shawndra's parents. In the last couple of years, Lady Jeanine had taken Sebastian, and occasionally Shawndra, on her shorter trips.

Shawndra's parents were bakers, and her father would make sweet bread in the shape of all sorts of animals for the children to play with, and then eat. She loved delivering food to the Citadel. Not because she liked baking, she actually hated working inside a house and in the kitchen. What she did love was watching the soldiers being trained under Captain Hart's diligent command. He was tall and commanding and seemed as though he could van-

quish any manner of man or beast. Even though she
knew there had never been a woman trained as a soldier at the Citadel, she would remember what the
Captain would tell his men and then she would go
home and practice it at night when her parents were
asleep. She had learned how to attack and defend
with a hardened loaf of bread. She also learned to
mask her movements so her opponent would not
know how she intended to strike. This came in
handy when she was occasionally picked on by older
boys. There were many boys in Crespin who have
had their face bloodied by an unsuspecting strike to
the bridge of the nose. None of them dared to tell on
her because they didn't want to be known as the boy
who was whipped by the baker's daughter.

Sebastian asked, "Are you delivering food to the
Citadel again?"

Shawndra replied, "Yes, do you have enough
food with you?"

"Yes, Lady Jeanine packed me a meal of bread,
cheese, and meat."

"It sounds like the perfect meal after a long day-
dream," said Shawndra. She gave Sebastian a knowing
look that made him blush again as they walked back
to the herd with the stray sheep in front of them.

"There's that fool horse!" came a voice from
behind them. It was Mr. Levert. He was stepping
quickly and hard as he approached Sebastian and
Shawndra. "That dumb animal has gotten out of his
stall for the fifth time in three days and every time

he makes his way toward you Sebastian. I don't even know how he gets out. I've locked the stall, placed heavy things against the door; it's beyond me how such a dumb animal can get out."

"Maybe he's not as dumb as we think he is," said Sebastian. Balam was close behind him with his head bowed low, as if he were trying to hide from Mr. Levert behind a thirteen-year-old boy.

Mr. Levert was a hard talking good hearted farmer. His father had been a farmer, his grandfather and great grandfather as well. Mr. Levert knew the land and the planting seasons. He could take a handful of dirt and tell you if it needed ash and how much it would need in order to produce the best crops. He could also smell the wind and tell you if it would rain that day. He was an exceptional farmer, and Sebastian liked him.

"I would think that shows the intelligence of an animal that he can get out of a stall that you have worked so hard to lock," said Shawndra with a smirk on her face. "Maybe we aren't as smart as we think we are."

"Well, smart or dumb, we will see who has the last laugh. I'm selling him to Farmer Caine down river."

"You can't do that!" said Sebastian in a panic. "I've seen his animals; they are all skinny and overworked. Please don't sell Balam to him," pleaded Sebastian. The horse lowered his head and moved closer to Sebastian as if to signal that he didn't want to go any more than Sebastian wanted to see him go.

Farmer Caine didn't have respect for animals and

the land like Mr. Levert. Mr. Levert was hard but fair. Mr. Caine was just hard. Sebastian had seen him whipping his poor beasts through the fields when they were tired and had not had enough water. Sebastian couldn't bear the thought of gentle Balam being treated that way.

"Balam," said Mr. Levert in surprise. "Since when does he have a name?"

"I didn't want to just call him 'horse,'" said Sebastian. "Besides, he's always seemed like he's wanted to say something. And you must admit, he is rather smart for a horse."

"Well, I need an animal that can work, and this one's too stubborn to plow, too smart to stay put, and too expensive to keep," said Mr. Levert, as he took a small towel from his belt and wiped his head.

"Why don't you let me buy him?" asked Sebastian. Sebastian surprised himself with the offer, and Shawndra looked surprised as well.

"If you want to buy this stubborn horse, then be my guest. However, since Farmer Caine has offered six silver pieces for the beast, I won't accept any less. It will help make up for the food he's eaten."

"Give me a day to raise the money, and I'll be back tomorrow for the horse," said Sebastian. He didn't know where or how he would get the money, but he knew he had to.

"Very well, I'll see you tomorrow." Mr. Levert smiled. "Though I doubt you'll be able to raise six silver pieces in one day. I only pay you five copper coins for a day's work. However, here's what I'll do. You take the horse home with you for the night, and I'll give you the rest of the day off to raise the money. Is that fair, Sebastian?"

"Oh yes," said Sebastian, who was very excited about the prospect of leaving the sheep early. "That is very fair." Sebastian and Shawndra took Balam and retrieved Shawndra's cart that was being pulled by her family's pony because it was loaded down with all sorts of food for the soldiers. Sebastian, Shawndra, and Balam headed for the Citadel.

———·——

The Citadel was built at the opening to the generous quarry that was Falls Lake and the city that surrounded it. The city was deserted since the large falls churned up a mist from the dead water that would make any creature sick if they breathed too much of it. However, the Citadel was far enough away that it was safe.

It was difficult to imagine that once there was a great city at Falls Lake that was bustling with merchants. Falls Lake was called the Light of Crespin, and people would come for a yearly pilgrimage to seek the Elders' wisdom and bathe in the nourishing waters. But all the Elders, save only one, had departed, and no one had sojourned there for over ten years. The Citadel that once defended the city was now there to keep wanderers from venturing into the falls. It seemed that the light of all Crespin had faded into an oily haze that everyone would rather forget. Falls Lake was now a monument to their faded glory.

As Sebastian and Shawndra approached the gates of the Citadel with their pony and cart in tow, Shawndra began to speak. "I think it is unfair that only men may be trained as warriors. Shouldn't women be given the choice of helping to defend their homes with more than just sewing needles and rolling pins?"

"I suppose so," said Sebastian, because he feared a bloody nose more than disagreeing with her. Besides this was a regular conversation with Shawndra. She had a lot of passion and plenty of courage with no way to show it except by bringing food every week to those who had permission to train.

"Not all men make the best warriors or the best spies. Wouldn't you agree, Mr. Bolo?" Shawndra then turned to a hedge on the side of the road and glared at it as if she were expecting it to speak.

A loud clank came from the bush as a voice from inside of it said, "Oh bother, I've dropped my sword again." Then the bush began to shake violently, and a round young man of sixteen years fell out of it and rolled onto the road with leaves and twigs stuck in his hair.

Bolo got up and brushed the dirt and leaves from his squire's uniform and then retrieved his sword from inside the bush. "How did you know I was there?" Bolo asked. Bolo was slightly older than

Sebastian and Shawndra but they were all friends since childhood. When Bolo was fourteen he joined the Citadel to train to be a guardian. For the last two years, the Captain of the guard and his second in command, Ba'ar, drilled Bolo in the skills required.

"I smelled peppered dried beef," said Shawndra. "And since my father is the only one who makes it, and you're the only one in the Citadel that likes it, I figured that you were near. And you're not a good climber, so the steep cliffs ahead would not be a good place for you, so I guessed that you were behind the bush."

"That's great, Shawndra. I thought it was the horse I was smelling," said Sebastian.

Shawndra continued to look at Bolo as he stood there with his wrinkled and soiled uniform. "Remember what Captain Hart said, 'If you don't want to be noticed, don't have anything with you that is noticeable.' You need to keep your food sack closed tightly."

"How did you know he said that?" asked Bolo.

"He went over spying and tracking two weeks ago while I was preparing your food."

"Wow, I wish I had your memory," said Bolo. "I just can't seem to get the hang of this whole soldiery thing." Bolo enjoyed the studying part of being a guardian and he had a talent for strategy, but his skills at tracking and fighting needed some work. "Not only do I have to do my regular training, but the Elder Jeanine sends me other exercises to do."

"What sort of exercises?" asked Shawndra.

"Indeed, what sort of exercises, Bolo?" Sebastian, Shawndra, and Bolo all turned to look and saw standing there Ba'ar, Captain Hart's second in command of the Citadel. Ba'ar joined the Citadel when he was fourteen and has served the Captain for the past seven years. He was one of the first recruits to the Citadel after the dead water poisoned the falls and the older guardians became ill or fled. Ba'ar was skilled with a sword and had little patience for Bolo or anyone else.

"Just some riddles and puzzles she asks me to solve, Commander Ba'ar." Bolo had never mentioned this to anyone at the Citadel and regretted that Ba'ar knew now. Ba'ar always acted like he resented Bolo because he was so slow to learn the ways of the sword. However, Bolo routinely scored at the top of his class in battle strategy. Captain Hart commented that Bolo made the highest marks he had ever seen in the history of the Citadel when it came to organizing and planning for battle. Shortly after that, Ba'ar seemed to single out Bolo even more in front of the other squires to humiliate him in single combat. It was if he was trying to prove to others, as well as himself, that he was better than Bolo.

"I don't know why the last remaining Elder would waste her time with the likes of you. She would be better off training our other squires that have the potential for making the rank of knight," said Commander Ba'ar.

"Why haven't you made knight, Mr. Ba'ar?" asked

Sebastian. He asked because he knew the answer, and the answer would get Ba'ar to stop picking on Bolo.

"Because a squire must go on a quest and also prove himself in real combat. Those are two things Mr. Ba'ar hasn't done," said Shawndra with a tone that showed her contempt for bullies.

Ba'ar walked quickly forward to the two thirteen-year-olds and stood over them as to highlight the difference in size upon them. "First of all, it isn't Mr. Ba'ar, It's Commander Ba'ar. Second of all, there hasn't been a war or combat in Crespin for over thirteen years. And third, any time you want to challenge my skills, I welcome the challenge, children." Ba'ar almost spat out the last word as he stood defiantly with his left hand resting on the hilt of his sword on his left hip.

Ba'ar wore the insignia of the Commander of the Citadel proudly. The insignia was a medallion with an inscription on the outer border that read, "Faith in each other. Hope for the future. Love for justice." In the center of the medallion was an image of the Citadel. This medallion was fastened to a heavy gold chain that went around the neck. It was a good contrast with his silver armor chest plate, chain mail sleeves and burgundy cloak and hood that were fastened about his shoulders. Commander Ba'ar always seemed very fashionable in his armor and spent many hours polishing the metal to a high shine.

"Call me a child again, and you'll see that…" Shawndra began as she made her fists, preparing to add another person to her list of bloody-nosed victims.

"I think it's time we get this food to the Citadel. We don't want any guardians to go hungry," interrupted Sebastian. He knew that this confrontation would not end well if it continued to progress.

"Yes, children, you need to run along and deliver our food. I would hate to have to cancel your parent's contract because their foolish little daughter doesn't know when to keep her mouth shut," said Ba'ar to Shawndra. He knew that the Citadel was the main source of business for Shawndra's parents.

"Let's go, Shawndra. There's no point to staying here. Will you come with us, Bolo?" asked Sebastian.

"No, he cannot. He has work to do here," said Ba'ar.

Bolo looked to the ground and said in a lowered voice, "You had better go on without me, Sebastian. I'll be here."

Sebastian whistled for Balam, and he came trotting around the corner almost running over Ba'ar. This pleased Shawndra and made her like the horse even more. She took her pony that was pulling the food cart and began to walk toward the Citadel again. They could hear Ba'ar's voice well after they turned the corner shouting commands at Bolo.

"I just don't know how someone like Ba'ar can be entrusted with the care of young cadets. He loves his position but seems to hate anyone of lower rank, especially poor Bolo," said Shawndra with a huff.

"I agree, but it doesn't do you any good to antagonize him that way because he will probably be the next Captain of the Guard after Captain Hart steps down," said Sebastian.

"Thankfully that won't be anytime soon. It takes more than a strong sword and hot temper to command troops. It takes a strong heart and mind, and our Bolo has both of those. I don't think Ba'ar could get out of a problem that didn't involve hacking at something with a blade," Shawndra said in a laugh.

"Let's put Ba'ar behind us because the Citadel is just ahead," said Sebastian.

As Sebastian and Shawndra rounded the corner, they saw the walls of the Citadel. It was a journey they had made often, but every time the Citadel came into view, they were awestruck with the size and grandeur of the guardian of Falls Lake.

THE CITADEL

Sebastian and Shawndra walked along the path cut out of the walls of the quarry while being very mindful not to get too close to the water's edge. The path had once been a wide road that was well kept with precisely cut stones so that carts and animals could travel through the entrance to Falls Lake without a fuss. In the walls were carved places for people to stand out of the way of traffic. Sebastian assumed it was because there was the occasional large buggy that could run someone over if they didn't have a place to jump out of the way. Today the road was littered with loose boulders and rocks, and much dirt had piled up against the edges from wind and rain that made the path narrower. Some brambles and prickly bushes had grown up between the paving stones because they were the only things tough enough to withstand the stench of the dead water.

As Sebastian and Shawndra rounded the final turn, they saw what inspired merchants with awe and intimidated wrong doers with fear. The great and inspiring façade of the Citadel. The high walls of the Citadel were smooth and unscalable. The very shape of the fortress seemed to whisper a warning into the souls of travelers, "Beware, for I am watching!" On the highest parapet was a solitary squire. His station was to warn the garrison of invaders. Today, he alerted the few other guardians that the food was arriving.

Sebastian and Shawndra led their cart, pulled by the donkey and followed by the young colt, to the entrance of the Citadel. They walked by the heavy iron gate that had not been closed in many years. The entrance was under a long tunnel on the inside of the Citadel. The large arching door was heavy and made from ironwood. The two could hear the quick shuffling of footsteps of young guardians running down the stone steps to help Shawndra unload the cart and attempt to hide in their capes loose pieces of cheese and dried venison.

"This is probably where we should go our separate ways," said Sebastian. "You're about to have all the help you need, and I have to get to Lady Jeanine and talk to her about Balam." Sebastian took Balam's reins and began walking toward the end of the tunnel that marked the entrance to Falls Lake.

"Sebastian," Shawndra called out, "I do hope you get to keep Balam. He really is an exceptional horse."

Sebastian smiled and waved as he turned onto his path that would lead him to the house where he and Lady Jeanine lived. He could hear Shawndra's voice echoing off of the walls as he left. She was giving instructions to the young squires on how to carry the food best, as well as issuing threats to anyone who would attempt to keep a rogue sliver of bread for himself.

Shawndra marched up the stairs into the heart of the Citadel, and the young squires helped her bring the food supplies to the main kitchen. She was putting away the bread, cheeses, and dried meats in the cupboards in a fashion that the soldiers could easily find them. There was no cook that lived at the Citadel, so the youngest squire had kitchen duty on a regular basis.

The kitchen was high up in the Citadel, and Shawndra could see through an opening in the stone wall to the main room. The room was used for both eating and teaching. It was a large gallery with high ceilings and a wood floor. The walls were stone, and the floor had knot holes in it where over time heavy platters or semi-sharp axes had been dropped and gouged deep gaps in the boards. In the gallery sitting around the tables were a couple of young apprentices who had just finished practicing knife fighting and were resting. Often Shawndra thought that cadets did too much resting and not enough practicing. She could hear their conversation and wished she had arrived earlier to see the practice.

She knew each of the young men well. They were kind enough and learned not to harass Shawndra too badly. They might find some sand, a rat's tail, or something worse in their bread if they were too coarse with her, not to mention a quick jab to the ribs that would leave her victim breathless. She always seemed to know just where to strike them that got past their armor and straight to a nerve. Nevertheless, a small degree of torture on the cadet's part was expected.

One of the young soldiers was Kelli. He was the newest to the Citadel but was a fast learner. He was almost seventeen years old with brown hair and bright eyes. The other cadet was twenty-two years old and one of Captain Hart's most trusted squires in the training of the young ones. His name was Ethan, and Shawndra knew him to be very patient. She also noticed that he had more than an average skill with a knife.

Ethan and Kelli were laughing and talking about their practice when Kelli noticed that one of the knot holes was big enough for his entire big toe. When he placed his toe through the knot hole it looked as if his toe had been cut off completely. Kelli looked at Ethan and said, "I'll begin to shout and say that you dropped your sword and it fell on my foot and cut my toe off. You go get the other squires and when they come in here they will all panic and then we will have a good laugh at the rest of the boys."

Ethan looked at Kelli and rolled his eyes and said, "Oh sure, that'll work just fine. I'll go get the boys, and you sit there with your toe in the floor." As he walked away from Kelli he saw Shawndra through the entrance to the kitchen. He walked in and said, "Hello, Shawndra."

"Hello, Ethan," said Shawndra. She was startled because she fancied him. Ethan had always been kind to her and corrected any of the boys that tried to pick on her. He was also one of the best soldiers at the Citadel. All the other boys talked big and tall about themselves, but they couldn't match the skill of Ethan. In Shawndra's opinion, the only difference between Ethan and Ba'ar was that Ethan was kind to people and didn't feel the need to tell others about how good he was.

"I hear that Kelli gave you a terrible time last week when you brought the food in," said Ethan in a hushed voice so that no one outside the kitchen could hear.

Shawndra replied, "Yes, but that's to be expected from boys. I thank you for not doing the same. You and the Captain never give me any trouble."

Ethan leaned close and said, "Maybe you might be interested in giving a little trouble yourself?" He grinned a devilish grin that said he was devising a delightfully wicked plan. Shawndra wanted to know more.

"What do you have in mind?" she said as she put down the bread and leaned close, not wanting to miss a thing.

"If a person wanted to teach Kelli a lesson, that person could go downstairs to the room directly beneath the gallery and see that Kelli has put his toe through a hole in the floor above," said Ethan. "If that person took a piece of stove wood with them from the kitchen and stood on the table, they could give Kelli's toe a good whop.

Shawndra almost squealed with excitement. This was unusual because Shawndra was never known to squeal. Even when two boys dropped some spiders in her hair once, she did not squeal. But this was too delicious, too fun not to get excited.

"Yes, a person could do such a thing, couldn't she?

"Yes, she could," said Ethan quietly. "Now I have to go and get the other boys and let Kelli play his game." Ethan turned and walked out of the room and called for the other cadets and squires. Shawndra turned and could see from the kitchen into the great room that Kelli was too preoccupied with his toe that was in the hole to notice the scheming looks that had passed between Ethan and herself. Shawndra turned to the stairs and grabbed a stick of round stove wood and darted out of the room and down the stairs to the lower level.

When she found the room that had a toe sticking through the ceiling, she pulled a small table underneath it. Shawndra jumped up on the table and realized that she was too short. Panic set in that she would not be able to accomplish such a delicious bit of mischief just because she hadn't grown enough.

She immediately jumped off of the table, found a chair in the next room and then placed it on top of the table. When she stood on it she then knew that with the length of the stove wood, she would be able to give Kelli's toe a mighty whop.

Shawndra waited until she heard the footsteps of what had to be the other squires entering the room. She heard Kelli's fake cries of pain and Ethan's less than convincing attempts at going along with the joke. Shawndra lifted the round piece of stove wood and swung hard. The thud it made against the wood and toe was loud but not nearly as loud as the squeal let out by Kelli. His scream of pain was now very convincing. And Ethan's cries of laughter were very genuine. The toe disappeared from the hole, and Shawndra could see the occasional face of squires looking in the hole with faces twisted in laughter. She delighted in the prank and wanted to run immediately to find Sebastian and Bolo and share all the juicy details.

Shawndra would not be able to tell anyone immediately because through the hole, just big enough to put a big toe through was now a solitary eye looking straight at her. She looked up and realized she had lingered there too long. Kelli's eye had met hers, and he knew just who to get revenge against. She heard him cry out, "Shawndra! Now you've done it. That almost broke my toe off. I'm coming down to get you right now. I'm gonna put you over my knee, little girl." She heard him get up and take one step, and then she heard a large crash on the floor and more laughter from everyone else in the room.

Ethan said, "And how are you going to catch her when you can't even take two steps without falling down?"

"I don't need to run on both feet to catch one small girl," said Kelli. Then Shawndra heard a loud thump, thump, thump sound on the floor, and she knew that Kelli was making his way to the stairs to come down and find her. Shawndra jumped off of the chair on the table and then jumped to the floor. In a flash, she had made it to the stairs and rounded the corner just in time to be out of reach of Kelli as he was coming after her. He lunged to catch her and missed. Shawndra was racing down the stairs as she heard the cries of Kelli behind her, mixed with the clanging of his armor as he rolled down the stone steps. She laughed to herself as she reached her cart that was tied up outside of the Citadel. She quickly untied her pony and began her journey back home. She knew she had won another victory and any boy that would see her as a victim of their humor would now think twice before picking on her.

Sebastian and Balam rounded the corner that would take them to the house of Lady Jeanine, the Elder. She could usually be found this time of day sitting just outside the front door on a small bench waiting for Sebastian to return. She always greeted him with a warm smile and a list of questions about his day. She would then tell him that she had made his dinner, and they would go inside the house, sit at the table, and eat together. She never seemed to be surprised at the time he came home. Whether he came home late or early, she was always there to welcome him.

As Sebastian approached the humble little house he was surprised that Jeanine had a guest. Normally when someone wished to speak to the Elder, she would sit at her bench while they stood in front of her or sat on the ground and spoke or listened, whichever was appropriate. The Elder was always in the place of honor. However, this time Jeanine was standing while a wild looking man was sitting on her bench. They were discussing something as the man rocked back and forth in a nervous fashion. His hair was dirty and tangled, as if it had not been brushed in some time. He wore animal skins with a leather belt that tied at his waist. This was the only thing that gave his body shape. It was difficult for Sebastian to tell what color his skin was because the man was so dirty.

Sebastian was at least thirty feet from them when he realized it was the same dirty crazy haired man that had saved him so many days ago when he had faced the wild dogs. Sebastian quickly darted behind some prickly bushes so that he would not be seen. Balam did exactly what Sebastian did, and Sebastian was thankful. Even though they were far apart, Sebastian could still smell the stench of a man that had not bathed in a long time.

Falls Lake was full of mysteries, and the deserted city with its empty doors and windows always gave Sebastian the creeps. There were times when young Sebastian felt as though he was being watched. Sometimes he thought he caught a glimpse out of the corner of his eye of a form looking from behind a tree or a boulder. But there was never anyone there. This dirty looking man fascinated Sebastian, so he hid himself and tried to move closer to find out what was going on.

The man was running his dirty fingers over a plate that apparently Lady Jeanine had given him full of food. He was wiping the last of the crumbs off with his dirty hands and then almost placing his whole hand in his mouth. As the food was finished and the Elder took the plate, the volume of the man's voice raised considerably and he spoke in an excited fashion. He then pulled a dagger from underneath his cloak and held it in his hand. Sebastian shifted his weight forward and prepared to rush in to defend his old friend. However, in that moment he saw a hand signal from Lady Jeanine that told him to remain hidden and not to move. He and the old lady had a secret language that only they shared. If she wanted to communicate something to Sebastian from across the room without anyone else knowing, she could use a combination of hand gestures and eye movements to tell him exactly what she wanted him to do.

It didn't surprise Sebastian that Jeanine knew he was there. Even though she wasn't facing him, she was aware of his presence and sent her signal to him by reaching behind her back and signaling him with her hands. Sebastian moved back into hiding as the wild man handed the knife to Lady Jeanine, and she humbly took it and placed it inside her cloak. Jeanine took one step back and bowed low as the man stood from the bench.

Sebastian was amazed by this interaction between the very noble Lady Jeanine and the wild, smelly man. If anything, the man should bow to the lady. She was obviously more important, especially since she was the last of the Elders. However, it was she that bowed deeply as the man stood from the bench and looked around nervously, as if sensing that he had stayed too long. With a few quick words the man hunched over and ran on the path that led deep into Falls Lake. *What a foolish path to take*, thought Sebastian. *If any man or beast stays in the falls area for very long they will become very ill from the mist of the dead water and be overcome. And anyone who wishes to rescue them will have the same fate.*

Lady Jeanine turned and looked at the grey brittle prickly bushes that Sebastian was hiding behind and called to him, "It's all right now, young Sebastian. You may come out." Lady Jeanine met Sebastian with the warm smile that he had come to expect. Her eyes were very alive, and her face seemed to brighten the dullest of rooms. Her voice held strength, even if her body was old and frail looking. Some elderly people that Sebastian had spoken to sounded as if they had resigned their lives to waiting for death. The light of their youth had long faded and the atrophy of many years of inactivity had taken over their bodies. But not Lady Jeanine. She was very much alive. When she desired it, she could race him down the path to the Citadel. It had only been in recent years that Sebastian was able to win these short races. He had also never known the Elder to be sick or ill. She was the only parent Sebastian had ever known, and he loved Lady Jeanine dearly.

"What was that about?" asked Sebastian as he approached the small house where he and Lady Jeanine had lived since before he could remember.

"That, my dear Sebastian, is a good question." She smiled at Sebastian and turned to walk into the house. "Now after you give that colt some hay, oats, and water from the shed out back, come inside and have some food. I suspect we have some things to talk about."

The colt! thought Sebastian, as if it were screamed in his mind. The sight of the old man and the lady talking made Sebastian forget about Balam. Sebastian turned back on the path to the Citadel and ran around the prickly bush to find his young horse. There was Balam standing exactly where Sebastian had dropped the reins. For once the colt didn't follow him. Balam could have given away Sebastian's position if he had made any noise. This further convinced Sebastian that this young horse had good sense.

Sebastian took Balam's reins and led him behind the house where he and Lady Jeanine lived. There, surprisingly, Lady Jeanine had set out oats and hay and had brought some drinking water from inside the house and prepared a place or Balam. "One of these days I'm gonna find out how she knows all these things before I tell her," said Sebastian to Balam. He took off the colt's bridle and bit so that Balam could eat and drink. Sebastian then closed the gate to the small courtyard that was just the right size to keep a small horse.

Sebastian went inside the house to find Lady Jeanine sitting in her usual chair next to the plate she had prepared for him. She had made him some stew from the leftover rabbit they had the night before. There was a fresh loaf of bread with some water. As Sebastian sat down, he gave thanks to the Great Mai for the provision of the food. This was a tradition that Lady Jeanine had taught him. She spoke of the time before the dead water as a time of plenty when all of Crespin was flourishing with prosperity and growth. She said it was important to remember where all their great fortune came from and to be thankful for everything they received. Sebastian didn't know of this time because for his whole life the waters of Crespin were poison. But he still maintained the tradition of giving thanks because it pleased the Elder.

"Tell me about your horse. Does he have a name?" asked Jeanine.

"Yes, his name is Balam, and he belongs to Farmer Levert. I helped with his birth a couple of years ago, and ever since he's followed me everywhere, even when he's not supposed to," said Sebastian.

"He looks like a strong animal. Do you think he can carry a heavy pack for a long distance?" asked the lady as she leaned forward as if she was very interested in Sebastian's reply.

"Well, Farmer Levert hasn't been able to get him to plow, but he has carried me on his back with no trouble several times."

"The time is drawing near when we will need some help with those sorts of things," said Jeanine. She produced from her cloak a small leather pouch and placed it on the table in front of Sebastian. "In that pouch are six silver coins. That seems the fair price for a good colt. Take that to Farmer Levert early in the morning and then return here as quickly as you can. We have many preparations to make." Sebastian was excited and surprised all at the same time.

"That's wonderful!" he shouted. "That's the exact price that Farmer Levert had asked for Balam. Oh my lady, that is great news. I will go in the morning and give him the coins." It was then that in Sebastian's excitement that he remembered the rest of what Lady Jeanine had said.

"Preparations for what?"

"Good, you didn't let your enthusiasm make you forget your good sense," said Jeanine with a smile and small chuckle. She stood up out of her chair and retrieved a parchment scroll from the shelf where she kept most of her books and papers. She laid it on the table and rolled it out flat. Sebastian recognized what it was immediately.

"It's a map of all of Crespin," he said.

"Yes Sebastian, that's exactly what it is," said Jeanine. "The day after tomorrow we will leave on a journey unlike any we have ever made."

Lady Jeanine had taken Sebastian on many trips that involved walking several days. Two of their journeys had traveled the Agriplaines to the Cedar Forest to see the massive trees. There they even caught a glimpse of the Podo people as they walked in and out of the deep forest.

Lady Jeanine and Sebastian had traveled to Crescent City to see the bazaar and market places where people were bartering and selling their wares. The pace of Crescent City was in sharp contrast to that of Falls Lake and the Citadel. Falls Lake was a dead ghost town while Crescent City was the largest city in Crespin and very much alive.

The Elder had even taken Sebastian to the entrance to the Valley of Dry Bones. A place that everyone avoided at all costs. No one ever spoke of what it was like in the valley because no one who went there ever returned. Lady Jeanine seemed to be the only person who was not afraid of what was in the valley and actually looked upon it with comfort and a sense of longing.

"Where will we go this time? Will we go south all the way to the ocean, to the Cajust Shoals? I've never seen a Creolus person. I've heard they are lizard riders," said Sebastian excitedly.

"No, Sebastian, we will not venture south again. This time we will go north," said Lady Jeanine.

"North?" said Sebastian. He looked at the map and saw that the northernmost city was Sodorrah. The only thing north of that was impassable granite mountains. Sodorrah was built by fishermen in the fork of two great rivers. It was the northern most point in the land of Crespin.

"So, we will go to Sodorrah?" asked Sebastian in a puzzled way. Since Falls Lake was the only known passage to the north, no one traveled to there or from there. There had been no commerce or communication with the people from the north since the dead water came. Sebastian and Lady Jeanine would have to walk the path that was cut into the rock on either side of the falls in the city of Falls Lake. However, since the dead water churned up a great poisonous mist, no man or beast could make the trip without being overcome by a great sickness. The sickness caused by the dead water was not only physical but seemed to reside in the soul as well.

"Actually," said the lady, "we will go even beyond Sodorrah. We will go where no maps lead. We will travel to the source of the spring that feeds the waters of Falls Lake. There we will see what has made the waters turn to poison, and maybe even return the waters to the way they were."

Lady Jeanine's words hung in the air as Sebastian

was struggling to understand what was just said. "I don't understand, my lady. How can we travel so far north? We can't even get past the falls. If we get within sight of the mist then we have gone too far. And even if we get past them, we will be too sick to travel the long journey to Sodorrah. And then…" Lady Jeanine stopped Sebastian by placing her hand gently on the top of his head as she stroked him caringly.

"Do not fear, sweet Sebastian. This is a journey that we have been planning for a long time. It's a journey that must be taken. One that you must make with me. All will be revealed in the fullness of time."

Sebastian's head was buzzing with questions. He wanted to know more, but he didn't know where to begin. "When you said, 'We have been planning,' who is 'we'?"

"The man you saw sitting on my bench this evening, he and I have been waiting for you to be old and strong enough to make the trip. It will be a long and perilous journey so we will need some help. I will take care of that in the morning when you go to pay Farmer Levert for the horse," said Jeanine.

Sebastian then remembered the words of the wild man when he had saved Sebastian's life on the Agriplaines, "Grow wise, boy, grow strong. Your time is coming." Sebastian now knew that he would see this man again. He would see this man many times again.

"Who will you get to go with us, and how long will the trip take?" asked Sebastian. He had stopped eating and forgotten anything other than what he and Lady Jeanine were speaking of at that moment.

"As for who we will take, we will take all who must go," she said with a knowing smile. "As for how long it will take, not a moment more than the journey requires." Lady Jeanine knew these kinds of answers did not satisfy other people's curiosity, but she had found that with every answered question, there were dozens of new questions. Besides, it was healthy to have a sense of adventure and to step out on a journey in faith.

"Now Sebastian, no more questions. Tomorrow will take care of itself, and we have many things to do. I don't suspect that you will sleep tonight, but I must." Lady Jeanine leaned over to Sebastian as he was still sitting in his chair at the table with his food and the map of Crespin in front of him. She kissed him on the forehead and said, "Good night, Sebastian." The Elder Jeanine walked back to her small room where she slept on a bed of animal furs. Sebastian didn't know how Jeanine would be able to make such a trip. That must be why she was willing to pay for Balam, she needed to ride the horse to Sodorrah. But even an Elder would not be able to withstand the poisoned mist of the falls. For the first time in his life, Sebastian worried for the well-being of Jeanine. He didn't want to think of what life would be like if he lost her.

Sebastian's head was spinning, and he could no longer remain seated at the table. He heard a rustling in the courtyard behind the house and went to check on Balam. The horse was standing over the trough enjoying his meal of oats and hay. Sebastian went over and petted the neck of the gentle beast and spoke to him.

"Well, old friend, I think you picked the wrong time to switch homes. I thought I was saving you from being sold to a mean old farmer, but this trip may be the end of us both. I hope you will forgive me." Sebastian returned to the house and fell into his bed. Everything in the room now looked different to him, as if he were saying goodbye to the comforts of familiarity for the last time.

PREPARATIONS

Sebastian rose early in the morning to take the six silver coins to Farmer Levert in payment for Balam. His head was still spinning from all the things Lady Jeanine had told him the night before. *How will we travel north?* wondered Sebastian as he scratched his mussed hair. The mountains were full of creatures of great size and power. Legends were told from before the dead water came about the cities and animals that lived around and in the towering granite mountains. And all this was assuming they would even make it past the falls. The great unending flow of water was like a deadly veil that separated the north from the rest of Crespin. If anyone was to choose the most difficult and deadly undertaking in the land, this would be it.

Sebastian rode the young horse all the way to the farmer's house. Mr. Levert didn't look astonished when Sebastian handed him the money. He said, "Yup, your Elder friend was by here early this morning to let me know you were coming. She also told me that you wouldn't be back to shepherd for me for a while. Are you two going on a trip?"

"I guess so. When did she come by?" asked Sebastian.

"She came by just as I stepped out the door to tend my animals."

"Aren't you usually up at sunrise?" Sebastian was now amazed. If Lady Jeanine had traveled all the way to Farmer Levert's house before sunrise, she must have risen exceptionally early.

"I'm up before sunrise, young man. If you're ever gonna make it as a decent farmer, you gotta learn to wake up before the sun," said Farmer Levert as he stretched his back and smiled with pride.

"I'll keep that in mind. But for now I want to go tell Shawndra that I've bought Balam. She'll be very excited," said Sebastian as he took Balam's reins and began to turn the horse.

"Well, that's exactly where Elder Jeanine was headed. She said she had business with them." Farmer Levert held Balam's reins while Sebastian swung himself onto the horse's back. "I guess if you're headed somewhere, you gotta have something to eat. And that Baker family makes the best traveling food I've ever heard of."

"Do you think I can catch her if I ride hard all the way?" asked Sebastian.

"I don't know. Those Elders are known to be swift travelers. I don't see how they can get so far on foot though. They're all old and withered, but they got a fire in them," said Farmer Levert as he scratched his balding head.

"Well, I had better get going if I'm going to catch her," said Sebastian. With a firm pull of the reins and a nudge in Balam's side, the horse and his rider were on their way to see Shawndra. Sebastian tapped Balam with his heels but tried not to run him too hard. He knew that they would soon take a long journey, and he didn't need to wear the horse down before they left.

After a solid hour of riding, Sebastian arrived at the Baker's house. The smell of fresh rye and cinnamon bread was thick in the air. Sebastian could hear the raised voice of Shawndra's father. He was angry about something, and this surprised Sebastian as much as anything he had recently experienced.

Mr. Baker was a kindly man that was soft spoken and diligent about his work. Whenever Sebastian stayed with the Bakers while Lady Jeanine was on one of her journeys, Mr. Baker mostly stayed to himself. He would smile when their gazes would meet, but that wasn't often. In fact, he did little more for his own daughter and wife. He had a quiet strength and deep love for his family. When he spoke, it was in low murmurs and most people had to ask him to repeat what he said. It was his wife, however, that did most of the talking and selling in their bakery. He stayed busy at the brick oven while she chatted away with customers and bartered for eggs and meat.

But the raised voice of Shawndra's father was certainly unusual. Sebastian trotted the horse around toward the back of the Baker's home where the oven was located when he had to pull the horse to a sudden stop so that he didn't run over Mrs. Baker. She was scurrying away like a rat that was running from a cat. She looked up at Sebastian and said in a hushed voice, "Oh Sebastian, you don't want to go back there!"

Sebastian was even more surprised at Shawndra's mother's behavior. This was one of the loudest and most out going women he had ever seen. But today she was scared and mousy. "What is going on? Where is Shawndra? I wanted her to know that I have bought Balam and that I may also be going away with Lady Jeanine for a while."

"We know, Sebastian, we know. The Elder was here this morning just after sun up when my husband was starting the oven fire. She told us of her need for food for her journey north. She also told us that she was not going alone." After saying this, Sebastian could see tears forming in Mrs. Baker's eyes, though he wasn't quite sure why.

"It's fine ma'am; me and Lady Jeanine will be fine. We've traveled before, so there's no need to be upset. Why, once we went all the way to..."

Sebastian was not able to finish his thought when Mrs. Baker turned red and shouted, "What makes you think I'm concerned for you? Is that all you think about?"

Sebastian was speechless. He didn't know what was going on. What had Lady Jeanine done here that had wound this family up so tight? "Well, what are you sad about?" asked Sebastian, half-afraid of the answer.

"My little Shawndra is going with you. Didn't you know that?" At that moment, Mrs. Baker realized by the surprised look on Sebastian's face that he didn't know anything about it. In fact, this is the first he had heard of it. If Lady Jeanine was determined to pass beyond the falls, venture up river in dangerous terrain and put an end to the plague of the land, why would she choose a boy, a stubborn horse, and a small girl as traveling companions? Sebastian knew Elders didn't do anything without purpose, but this was beyond reason.

Sebastian's confusion was evidently written all over his face as Mrs. Baker moved close to him and touched him on his leg, as he was still mounted on the back of Balam. "You poor boy, you didn't know. And here I was, giving you what for when you don't even know the reason. I figured she took my little Shawndra because you needed a friend for the trip. But now I see that there is a different purpose." Mrs. Baker didn't seem to be comforted by this revelation, however she was calmed by it.

"When did she leave here?" asked Sebastian.

"Just a couple of hours ago. If you ride on to Falls

Lake, you should both get there at the same time," said Shawndra's mother. She clutched Sebastian's ankle so he would know she wasn't through talking with him. "Listen to me, Sebastian. My husband and I would never refuse Lady Jeanine anything. It's because of her that we even have little Shawndra. When Falls Lake was poisoned, I was about to give birth. I had gone there, as many of the women would do. Well, I went into labor before my husband could get me out. It was Lady Jeanine and her assistant that pulled me into her own home, and she helped me give birth. If it wasn't for her, little Shawndra would not have survived. Mr. Baker and I swore that we would do anything that the Elder asked. But this is too much. We can't give up our little miracle." Then Mrs. Baker moved even closer as to emphasize what she was about to say. "Sebastian, you have to convince the Elder not to take Shawndra with her. The trip upstream is deadly, and neither one of you have any business up there. Do you hear me? Don't go. Beg her not to go. Convince her to send my little girl back to me."

Sebastian's heart was heavy as he nodded his head in silence. He would try to convince Lady Jeanine not to let Shawndra go with them. He wasn't sure he wanted to go himself. Mrs. Baker released his leg, kissed her hand, and then placed it on his boot. "Ride to Falls Lake, Sebastian, ride now to save my little girl."

Sebastian pulled Balam's reins and nudged

the horse in the side and off they went across the countryside.

"Balam, I don't know what we've gotten ourselves into," Sebastian said with an empty look in his eyes. The horse took a quick step and whinnied as if he were trying to tell Sebastian something.

"You're right, Balam. This is no time for trotting. We have to go find Jeanine and Shawndra. Let's see how fast you can go." Sebastian moved forward on the horse's back and prepared to give him a kick when the horse broke into a sprint on his own. The horse and his rider darted across the Agriplaines. If one were looking on from a distance and couldn't see that Balam was an ordinary paint horse, they would swear that he was a thoroughbred practicing for the horse races in Crescent City.

Lady Jeanine and Shawndra were entering the narrow cavern that led into Falls Lake. Both of them had made this trip many times. They knew every bush, stone, and turn on the path that followed the Jezreel River into the canyon of the old ghost town. Even as a little girl, Shawndra wasn't very excitable. She had learned from watching the young men train in the Citadel under Captain Hart the discipline of silence. Captain Hart taught them that the more you show your opponent what you think, the more you tell them how to defeat you. All soldiers of the Citadel practiced this discipline by sitting face to face with

each other for hours without saying a word, yet trying to get the other person to talk. The first one to
talk had to withstand extra endurance trials.

Shawndra practiced this discipline on her own.
It made her parents worry because she could go
for days at a time without speaking a word. However, since she and the Elder left her house, she has
done nothing but idly chatter about everything and
nothing. "How long do you think it will be until
we get back home? Do you think we will see any
of the upland creatures that legends speak of? It's
a good thing my dadda gave me new boots, I will
need them for the trip. I never knew Elders could
walk so fast; I'm having to run to catch up."

Captain Hart could learn a thing or two from Elder
Jeanine about silence. She did not speak or whisper. Her bright and intense eyes did not give away
anything. She would smile warmly at Shawndra to
reassure her, but she just let her continue chatter-
ing away. Shawndra felt like a fool and wished that
she could stop gushing like a little girl. But she had
never been asked to go on a dangerous journey that
could potentially change the world.

"Shawndra, Lady Jeanine!" a faint voice was
heard in the distance. Shawndra turned toward
Lady Jeanine and saw a warm smile spread across
her face. She recognized the voice of the young boy
she had cared for since birth. The Elder didn't stop
or even slow down. She kept walking toward the
direction of the Citadel.

Shawndra turned and saw Sebastian sprinting toward them on the back of his new horse. Shawdra couldn't help but think, *He rides well for being bare back*. She was relieved to have someone with her that would speak to her.

Sebastian was panting and his knuckles had turned white because he was gripping Balam's mane so tightly. He had gripped the horse's sides as best he could with his legs so he wouldn't fall off. Sebastian had tried to stop Balam but had no success. It seemed that the horse wanted to get to Shawndra and the Elder as much or more than Sebastian.

"Balam, there they are. We made it to them just in time." Balam finally began to slow down. His coat was matted with sweat, and he was foamy around his neck. The horse slowed down more and eventually trotted up to Shawndra and then stopped. Sebastian slid off his back and staggered to his friend. "Your mother and father wanted me to convince you not to go with Lady Jeanine and me upriver."

Shawndra's face turned red as she placed her balled up fists on her waist and said with great force, "I am not going to just stay at home and let you and the last Elder in...in all of Crespin go off and explore everything without me."

Sebastian was surprised by Shawndra's reaction. "I don't want to leave you behind. I want you to come. But it's going to be dangerous, and there's no point risking two of us if we don't have to."

"Then why don't you stay behind?" said Shawn-dra as she narrowed her eyes and leaned forward.

"Well, I...I can't. I don't think." Sebastian knew that Lady Jeanine wanted him to go and didn't really give him a choice about the issue. The truth is he never thought to ask.

Shawdra turned back on the path that entered the canyon that led to the Citadel, and ultimately the ruins of Falls Lake and said over her shoulder, "Well, let's just go and ask the Elder who will stay and who will go." Shawndra's hair was flowing behind her because she was running so fast. The wind whipped through the canyon, and ordinar-ily Sebastian would barely even notice it, but today he and his horse had ridden hard and both were bone tired. Sebastian led Balam into the opening to Falls Lake, and they followed Shawndra as best they could. Sebastian didn't figure that even Balam could keep up with her at the moment.

What will I say to Lady Jeanine? wondered Sebastian. He thought that it might just be easier to get on Balam and ride away from this adventure. *What can I do that will change the way things are?*

As Sebastian pondered these things, his legs slowed more and more. Eventually it seemed as though they were standing still on the path. Balam whinnied and pushed Sebastian with his nose. "Why are you so excited about taking this trip? It won't be any safer for horses than for people!" The horse walked around Sebastian and continued on the path to the Citadel by himself.

"This is crazy," said Sebastian as he stood with his hands on his waist watching Balam continue on his own. "That horse has more courage than I do." A smile spread across his face as he realized he was being silly. Sebastian broke into a run to catch up with Balam. Once he caught up with him, Sebastian took the horse's reins and said with a laugh, "Okay, I get it. Let's go and face the Elder together."

The two walked on together until they turned the last corner that marked the entrance to the Citadel; there Sebastian saw an odd sight. Lady Jeanine was standing at the entrance to the Citadel with Shawndra at her side. They were speaking with Captain Hart in a very formal tone. Both Ba'ar and Bolo were standing at attention. Ba'ar towered over Bolo and seemed to dislike being paired with such a lowly looking soldier. Ba'ar was frowning, and Bolo was grinning so widely that the corners of his mouth could have tickled his ears.

Sebastian and the horse got close enough to understand what was being said. Jeanine was making preparations with Captain Hart and telling him why it was of the greatest importance that only those people she had chosen to be in the traveling party go upriver to Sodorrah and beyond.

"It has been written long before this day that these travelers, and these alone, would go to the source of the living water and remove this blight from the land." Jeanine's eyes sparkled with great intensity as she leaned forward, speaking with power and authority in her tone.

"I understand," said Captain Hart. "I've prepared for this day for years because you told me it would come. But the group you have chosen, are you really sure?" Captain Hart's concern was evident on his brow. The puzzled look on his face was something new to Sebastian. "There are many others to choose from. Let me—" Hart was never allowed to finish his sentence.

Lady Jeanine thumped her standard on the ground and said, "It must be these, Captain. This quest is not only for this age, but also for the age to come. There is much that we do not see, that will only be made known in the fullness of time." Lady Jeanine took a step toward the Captain and looked up at him and said, "We must trust the wisdom of the Great Mai. He is the only one whose vision is complete."

"I will do as you say," said Hart. The look of confusion left his face, and the firm, strong look of the Captain of the Guard returned. Hart turned to Ba'ar and Bolo and said, "Make preparations for a three day hike to Sodorrah. Pack provisions from the kitchen and wear your light armor. We leave tomorrow at first light, just as the Elder has spoken." Hart spun around and entered the Citadel disappearing through the iron gates. Ba'ar exhaled heavily and looked at Bolo, who was still standing at attention with his very unsoldierly grin.

"Wipe that smile off of your face," said Ba'ar as he stood over Bolo. Bolo's face dropped immediately as he realized that a three-day hike on an adventure upriver also meant three days of close contact with Ba'ar. "You're too simple to understand that this mission should not be given to lesser men like yourself. I would choose any of the others in the Citadel over you."

The pointed end of an ornate staff that had many carvings struck Ba'ar lightly on his breastplate, and he turned to look at the elderly woman who had caught his attention. Lady Jeanine looked at him intently with a raised eyebrow and said, "But you, young soldier, did not choose this group. For that matter, neither did I. It was the great king under the mountain that has chosen us all. Fortune and ruin await all of us up the Jezreel River; which part of that will be yours, I wonder?"

Ba'ar pushed her staff away and said with a grin, "I care not for your outdated beliefs. They did not save Falls Lake, and they have not purified the river. However, this is the first quest since the dead water came where a soldier of the Citadel may gain knighthood. I will have glory, and I will be a knight. Then I will return to my father's house and we will rule...I mean, we will serve the people together." Ba'ar had said too much, but it was nothing that the Elder didn't already know. The house of Ba'ar wanted power. Ba'ar's father, Halal, would see to it that they had it. Ba'ar's face was flushed, and he left Bolo, Jeanine, Sebastian, and Shawndra outside the Citadel.

Shawndra said, "That didn't sound very good."

"No dear, not good at all," said Jeanine, still looking toward the path that Ba'ar took into the Citadel.

"But that is not for us to be concerned with at this time. We have far more pressing matters to attend to." Lady Jeanine turned and looked at Sebastian and her cold, stern countenance turned instantly to a warm smile. "Now, you have ridden hard all this way to convince me to not let Shawndra go with us to Sodorrah, is that right?"

Sebastian was not surprised that the Elder knew what was on his mind before he spoke it. Sebastian nodded and said, "The Bakers, especially Mrs. Baker, pleaded with me to convince you to let her stay behind. After all, what can she bring that one of the soldiers cannot?"

Shawndra stepped forward to defend herself and argue for her place in the group when she felt the firm grip of the Elder on her shoulder. She felt her cheeks would explode as she stopped her words from spilling from her lips.

"As you have just heard me say to young Ba'ar, I did not choose this team. Walk with me, the three of you." Lady Jeanine motioned to Sebastian, Shawndra, and Bolo. "You as well, Balam." The horse whinnied and trotted behind the group as they walked toward the small house where Jeanine and Sebastian had lived for the past thirteen years. Jeanine began again, "The Great Mai has set this to be the time that we would journey past Sodorrah and onto the Veritasian Road to the source of the living water. And so, we must go at this time, or no other. Also, he has shown me that each of you must go with me as far as he leads. Not all of us will see the end, and none of us will return unchanged."

Shawndra tugged on Lady Jeanine's sleeve and asked, "So that means that I am going, right?"

Lady Jeanine laughed and said, "That means all of us are going. The six of us." Balam snorted loudly and stamped his hoof. "Pardon me," said Lady Jeanine, "the seven of us must go and fulfill the will of the great king under the mountain. Captain Hart will see to Bolo and Ba'ar being ready to leave in the morning, and I will make sure the two of you will be ready to go as well."

Bolo spoke up, saying, "I hope we get to see him. I've never heard of anyone that wasn't an Elder that has ever seen him. I wonder what he looks like. Is he tall or short, wide or thin, is he even a man or is he...are you okay, Sebastian?" Sebastian had frozen in place as they neared his house. Everyone looked at him and then looked in the direction he was staring and saw a figure of what looked like a man. A figure that was familiar to Sebastian and Lady Jeanine, but not to Bolo and Shawndra.

The wild looking, hairy man that had saved Sebastian from the wild dogs and had spoken to Lady Jeanine was standing before him. The man was between Sebastian and his home. He began to walk toward Sebastian at a quickened pace and reached inside the animal skin shirt that was held together with a worn chord. The wild looking man pulled a shiny thing from his shirt, and Sebastian could see that it was a jeweled dagger with a leather sheath. The man drew the blade when he was just steps away from Sebastian causing Shawndra and Bolo to gasp. Bolo reached for his sword and drew it so quickly that it flew from his hand and clanged on the pavement stones several feet from him. Shawndra squealed to Lady Jeanine, "Look out!"

Lady Jeanine moved quickly, but not in a manner that anyone anticipated. She quickly repositioned her feet and leaned forward, holding her standard and bowed very low to the man holding the dagger.

"Have you ever seen anything like this before?" said the smelly, wild man. He was now so close to Sebastian that the boy could feel the man's breath on his forehead. "Have you ever seen a blade that looks like this one?" The look in the man's eyes seemed as if he were barely holding on to sanity. Sebastian was too frightened to respond or even move. He thought that the man was surely going to run him through with the blade. Instead, the man held out the knife and scabbard, opened his palms and let them fall to the ground in front of him.

"Carry these close to you, young Sebastian. They will help you find your path." The dirty man began to step backward and then stopped. He looked past Sebastian and his eyes began to shine with tears. Sebastian turned and looked in the same direction and saw Captain Hart standing on the path. The Captain drew his sword, and Sebastian heard the wild looking man shuffle his feet quickly as if he were preparing to run and disappear inside the city. At least Sebastian knew one person that the wild man was afraid of. Sebastian looked to the Captain and saw him drop to one knee with his sword in front of him as if to salute the wild man. Sebastian wasn't close enough to say for sure, but he was almost positive a tear ran down Captain Hart's face. What could this wild man have done to deserve such respect and remorse from people such as Lady Jeanine and Captain William Hart?

Bolo and Shawndra were standing in astonishment at what had just occurred. The wild man turned and ran along the path leading into Falls Lake. Captain Hart rose, sheathed his blade and quickly returned to the Citadel. Lady Jeanine straightened, turned to Sebastian, and said, "Are you going to pick up that blade or let it lie there to rust?"

Sebastian picked up the small dagger and ran his fingers along the engravings at the base. There was an odd design on the hilt that looked almost like crooked teeth. "Why would I have seen something like this before?" asked Sebastian. Lady Jeanine smiled, and Shawndra reached out and took the blade from Sebastian to get a closer look.

"What an odd looking knife." Shawndra held it up to the light to let what was left of the sunlight glint off the shiny blade. "I've heard that when a dagger like this is made, it's because a sword was made first. They are a pair, you see."

Bolo stepped forward and asked, "So who has the

sword?" All three looked to Lady Jeanine, expecting an answer. She smiled, turned toward the house, and said, "It is time for Balam to be fed and for you three to eat some dinner.

"Oh dear," said Bolo. "I've got much to do tonight, and I can't miss dinner." Bolo turned and began to run down the stone path to the Citadel. He stopped, turned around and ran back past the small group, retrieved his sword, and placed it back in its scabbard. "I would appreciate it if you didn't tell anyone about this," he said as his cheeks turned red. Bolo then ran as best he could back to the Citadel where the evening lamps were being lit.

Shawndra said, "I really like Bolo, but he needs to work on his sword handling."

Lady Jeanine said, "Bolo will find his strength in due time. However, as for you two, we have a great journey to begin tomorrow, and that horse needs to be put up to rest."

Sebastian had almost forgotten about Balam. He took his reins and began leading him back to the stall where fresh hay, oats, and water had been prepared. "I'll brush him down and make sure he's taken care of," said Sebastian.

"I'll help you," said Shawndra. They both walked the horse into the small pen behind the house.

Lady Jeanine looked in the direction of the roaring black falls that were poisoning the remains of the forgotten city of Falls Lake. Her journey was about to begin, and the Elder could not see the end of it. She did not know if she would return. She only knew one thing for certain: she was to lead Sebastian and the others to the source of the spring. She trusted Mai, but the great king under the mountain had revealed nothing else to her. Lady Jeanine couldn't help but wonder if that was where her path would end. "So many words unsaid; so many deeds undone."

The sound of Sebastian and Shawndra laughing woke her from her melancholy dream. "Enough of this self pitying foolishness!" The Elder said to herself. "There are preparations to be made, and I must prepare myself for the journey." Lady Jeanine entered her small house and took a jeweled water flask from the mantle. She placed it in her private room and said, "Tonight I will drink deeply of the living water, for tomorrow our journey begins."

THE KING'S HIGHWAY

The morning began before the sun had peered above the granite canyon walls. The only sound of Falls Lake was the roaring water pouring over the falls. No bird or insect could live near the water, and so the sounds of spring, fall, winter or summer were all the same. No form of life heralded any change in Falls Lake.

Sebastian expected Lady Jeanine to roll him out of bed. He had gone to sleep on his cot, while Shawndra had gone to sleep on top of some animal skin blankets near the fire. Neither of them saw Lady Jeanine after they put Balam up for the night. The Elder had made food for them, packed their rucksacks for the next day, and then retired to her own room for the night. At one point, Sebastian was awakened by what he thought was a bright light coming from her room, but he assumed he was just dreaming.

Sebastian walked over to Shawndra and nudged her arm. "Wake up; it's time to get ready to leave."

Shawndra stirred and sat up and rubbed the sleep from her eyes. "Where is Lady Jeanine?"

"I don't know." Sebastian scratched his mangled hair and stretched his arms and legs. "I thought she would be waking us up. We may be up too early; it's not even light out yet."

"No, my dears," came a gentle voice from the darkest corner of the room. The amber coals in the fireplace gave off a dull light that did not have the power to chase the darkness from every corner. "You still have some time left before we must leave. You should try to sleep some more." The voice was familiar enough for Sebastian to know it was the Elder. However, there was something different about it. Something had changed, but he couldn't pin it down in his mind. Sebastian walked over to the large chair where he sat down and closed his eyes and drifted back to sleep. Shawndra lay back down and returned to her dreams. Neither of them suspected that in the light of the morning sun they would learn an amazing new truth about the power of the Elders.

Sebastian awoke again, but this time to the voices of Captain Hart, Ba'ar, and Bolo talking outside the door of their small house. Balam had whinnied as if to wake Sebastian so the young horse could have some familiar company. Sebastian slid out of his chair and shook Shawndra once again, and this time she did not wake slowly. She sat up quickly and said, "It's time, isn't it?"

"I suppose so," said Sebastian. Shawndra changed into her travel clothes that her mother had packed in Lady Jeanine's room, and Sebastian changed out of his night clothes in the main room. They both ate quickly from the dried fruits, jerked beef, cheese, and milk that Lady Jeanine had left for them on the table.

Sebastian and Shawndra stepped out of the door to see Balam loaded with sacks, harnessed and ready for the journey. Captain Hart, Ba'ar, and Bolo were wearing their light armor with swords and daggers strapped to their sides. The thick leather and chain mail armor was considerably less heavy than their dress armor that was thick plates of metal. Shields and spears were not for traveling, unless traveling to war.

Ba'ar was the first to speak to them. "Well, if it isn't our two sleepy adventurers. You're going to have to do better about waking up if you're going to travel with us." He smiled his crooked smirk at them and continued to check the packs they had loaded on Balam.

"I've packed enough food for all of us for a four-day hike to Sodorrah," said Bolo as he saluted Captain Hart. "I put a little extra in just in case it takes us a little longer to get there." The Captain of the Guard nodded at him and then turned and looked toward the dead city of Falls Lake.

"Has the Elder told us how we're gonna get

through that, Captain?" Bolo scratched his ear with an inquisitive look on his face.

"You'll know when we all know," said the Captain.

Ba'ar closed the top of his rucksack and said with a huff, "I don't like it. I mean, that Elder changing like that. I didn't know they had that power, and if she hasn't told us about that, what else has she not told us about?"

"You don't have to like it, Ba'ar, and there's nothing any of us can do about it," said Hart.

"Besides," piped in Bolo, "you were saying last night that because of her age, she would slow all of us down. Now you know she won't." Bolo chuckled and continued, "In truth, she may give us all a run for it now."

Ba'ar flushed red with anger and said, "Do not suppose to use my words against me, Cadet." Sebastian figured that the only reason Ba'ar didn't scream at Bolo was because Captain Hart was standing near. "I know my words and my thoughts. You just keep to what you're good at, and that's packing gear and eating too much food." Ba'ar stormed off toward the Citadel to make final preparations for leaving.

Sebastian and Shawndra overheard all of this and asked Bolo and Sebastian, "What do you mean the Elder has changed?"

Bolo's eyes raised and his chin dropped. "You mean you don't know? How could you have spent the night in her house and not known?"

"Known what?" said Shawndra who was growing impatient with all the vagueness of the moment.

"How could you have not known that she has changed...changed into a...a..." Bolo was searching for the right thing to say when a voice came from behind him.

"I'm glad to see that everyone is up and ready for an adventure." Sebastian and Shawndra turned to see a young woman walking out of the gate from behind the house. She was tall and beautiful. Her hair was as black as raven's feathers and was long, down to the middle of her back. Her features were delicate and strong as if her beauty hid a great power. She was dressed in light armor similar to the soldier's of the Citadel. But her armor was all black and had the design of a vine. She also had a long sword and a dagger at her side. Sebastian had never seen anyone that looked quite like her, but there was one thing that he did recognize. Those eyes were still as bright and powerful as ever. It was the Elder. Somehow Lady Jeanine had transformed into the young woman they saw before them. She no longer walked stooped over with age. She had no grey or wrinkle on her. The only things that remained were those sparkling eyes, her warm smile, and her voice.

"My lady!" said Shawndra as she knelt to the ground.

Lady Jeanine gave her familiar smile and said, "Get up, child. I am still the same today as I was yesterday, only with a few differences. You will not treat me any differently than you have in the past." Shawndra stood up straight but was still in awe of this powerful young yet ancient woman.

"And you, Sebastian," said Lady Jeanine as she stood in front of him. "What do you think about all this?" Lady Jeanine knew many secrets and hid them all well. But her concern for the boy was as evident as always.

"I can see that you are the same great lady I've always known. This will take some getting used to, but I guess I'll be fine with it." Sebastian smiled and was happy to know that even though the Elder had changed her appearance, it had not changed their friendship.

"This body is more suited for the sort of travel we will be doing," said the Elder.

"Excuse me, my lady," Bolo spoke up. "Begging your pardon, but how are you able to do whatever it is that you have done?" Bolo's awkward wording of his question showed his unease about the situation.

"I will tell you everything...well, I will tell you enough in due time," said Lady Jeanine. "The Elders have many secrets, and this is one of the least of them." Bolo, Shawndra, and Sebastian had heard from other people about the power of the Elders, but this was the first time they had ever seen a glimpse into just how powerful they might really be.

Ba'ar was returning from the Citadel with Ethan behind him. "Captain, the preparations are complete; all that is left is to turn over command of the Citadel to the new senior cadet." Ethan was in his formal armor, polished to a high shine. Captain Hart took a medallion from around his neck and stood in front of Ethan. Bolo and Ba'ar both stood at attention while Lady Jeanine looked on.

"Ethan, are you ready to accept this great responsibility?" asked Hart.

"Yes, Captain," said Ethan.

"You are now the temporary senior guardian of the Citadel. I charge you with the responsibility of continuing the training of the cadets, the security of the city of Falls Lake, and..." Captain Hart hesitated before completing his orders. Sebastian saw a flash of pain across his eyes as he continued. "...and the defense of the king." Hart finished and placed the medallion around Ethan's neck. Sebastian looked at Jeanine, and she returned a knowing look back to him. She had seen the flash of painful memory in the face of Hart. Sebastian figured this was one of the great secrets she carried with her.

Hart and Ethan exchanged salutes, and Hart picked up his rucksack and hoisted it up effortlessly onto his broad shoulders. Ba'ar and Bolo did the same.

"Well, there's nothing left but the leaving I guess," said Bolo.

"It is time," said Jeanine.

Balam whinnied as if to say he was ready as well. Sebastian and Shawndra picked up their rucksacks, and the six travelers and their horse began their walk into Falls Lake. Sebastian had only seen one person walk this path and that was the crazed wild man that had given him the dagger that he saw Lady Jeanine place in his sack. He wondered if they would all march into Falls Lake and then go just as loony as that man. Whatever was to happen, he remembered the words of Lady Jeanine from the day before. None of them would return unchanged.

———•———

The roar of the falls was getting louder and louder. Sebastian's heart was starting to beat harder as they approached the deadly mists that were churned up by the falls. He had never dared to venture this far into the city, and he was seeing the empty hulls of the buildings which were once homes for people that lived in a thriving city. There were many ornate carvings on the walls and pathways lining the city streets. He could see how this was once a great and beautiful city. But now all that was left were monuments to the death that awaited them in the heart of the city where the mists of the falls would poison their bodies and their very souls.

Lady Jeanine walked with her rhythmic tap tap tapping noise as she carried her same ironwood standard that Sebastian always knew her to have. She had carved many things on the standard. She would use it to tell Sebastian the history of Crespin and the Elders. She even had carved Sebastian's own name. She said she preferred to remember the day the dead water came as the day she was blessed with Sebastian. There were many marks on the standard that she would not explain. She would always say, "One day I may tell you that story, but only in the fullness of time." Sebastian hoped that he and all his friends would get to hear these stories, and that they wouldn't all be lost in the blackness that was brought on by being poisoned by the dead water.

The group turned a corner, and they were standing a short stone's throw from the entrance to the king's palace. The black mists of the falls were visible now, and they were very close. If they attempted to enter the palace, they would surely have to go through the deadly fog.

"We must enter the king's palace to find our path beyond the falls," said Lady Jeanine.

Ba'ar scoffed and said, "We cannot get any nearer to the dead water. You may have the power to heal yourself, but we do not."

Captain Hart turned and said, "Steady yourself, Ba'ar." Ba'ar straightened and stopped speaking, but it was obvious that he resented being silenced by Hart. The Captain turned to Lady Jeanine and said, "How do you propose we enter the palace and survive?"

While they were speaking, they didn't notice that Shawndra, while looking at the ornate paving stones had wondered closer to the mists. She was trying to make sense of the inscriptions when Ba'ar called out, "Look at that witless girl! She would wonder right into those mists if we let her."

Shawndra looked up and realized that she had wondered closer to the entrance to the king's palace and too close to the black mists. She turned and walked back to the group, a little embarrassed and a little scared. "I didn't get close enough to breathe any of the mists. I'm fine." She said the last words with a shaky voice as if she were not convinced of them herself.

Lady Jeanine, while looking at Shawndra, said, "Mr. Ba'ar, you asked how we will get into the king's palace without walking through the mists." Lady Jeanine smiled and said, "Like this." With her standard she tapped two pavement stones on the path, a tile on the wall and then put the end of the staff into a hole in the wall. A rumbling noise was heard, and a section of the wall in front of them parted, revealing a secret entrance from the street level into the palace.

Everyone but Captain Hart and the Elder gasped. It was obvious that Falls Lake held as many secrets as the Elder.

"There are many doors in Falls Lake; you just have to know how to open them," said the Elder. "Follow me; we are taking the king's highway." The lady turned and strode without fear into the dark tunnel. As the group began to follow her, they were surprised again to see torches light up the dark.

Bolo was leading Balam and was impressed that the horse didn't hesitate to follow them into scary places. Ba'ar didn't take his hand off of his sword. He stood ready to slash out in the darkness at any foe, real or imaginary. Sebastian and Shawndra stayed close to Lady Jeanine as well as Captain Hart.

The group came to the end of the tunnel, and Captain Hart pushed against the wall and it swung open. Everyone, including the horse, walked through the new opening and found themselves in the great rotunda of the palace. The rotunda was a round room with a high decorated ceiling and silver doors on the western wall. Columns surrounded the room next to the wall, and between each column was a painting of some significant event in the history of Crespin. They were all walking around and looking at the paintings when Ba'ar asked, "Is it safe to be in this palace, so close to the falls?" His voice trembled just a little, unmasking his unease at their present situation.

Lady Jeanine said, "I've never known you to be so concerned with safety, Ba'ar." Ba'ar became flushed and glared at the Elder. "You can rest assured," said the Lady, "we are quite safe here. The rotunda is far inside the palace, and those doors have been closed and sealed to the outside."

Captain Hart and Ba'ar were discussing something intensely military. Bolo was minding Balam, and Shawndra and Sebastian were walking around the room looking at the paintings. The first one of the series must have been Aaron the wanderer crawling into the valley that would one day be known as Falls Lake. The shadow of a Baruk behind him as he clutched his wounds gave that away. The next painting was of a king, a young boy, and a crowd of Elders laying the first stone of the city of Falls Lake. One of the Elders looked very similar to Lady Jeanine. Sebastian looked to her and realized that she was watching him. They smiled to one another in their familiar way. Sebastian thought to himself, *Even though she has changed her appearance, her heart is the same.*

Shawndra had moved on to the next painting and was trying to understand what it was about. It was of a group of men, all dressed in black with a peacock in the foreground. She thought, *That must be the judges of the Ivveleth. Only they would be so puffed up with themselves that they would be shown as peacocks.* Shawndra chuckled and then saw something odd. In the background of the painting looking out from behind a rock she saw the likeness of a small boy. Shawndra walked up close to the painting and studied his face thinking that it seemed familiar. The thin smile and devilish expression, she thought she had seen this before. As she stared closely, the boy in the painting seemed to look back at her and then suddenly he reached out of the painting to grab her.

Shawndra screamed as she threw herself back from the painting and scrambled to her feet. Sebastian was quickly at her side, and then Bolo, with his hand on his sword.

"What is it? What happened?" asked Sebastian.

Shawndra could barely speak, "The, the painting. It, well it sort of, I think it…"

"What did the painting do?" asked Bolo as he placed his hand on her shoulder to help steady her.

Sebastian said, "Just slow down and tell us what you saw."

"Well, I think the painting tried to grab me,"

said Shawndra. She was having difficulty believing herself.

They heard laughter from the far side of the room and turned and saw Ba'ar. "The painting tried to grab you? Oh, that's quite good. I guess that is why you are on this journey. To give us false alarms and entertain us with your imagination."

Captain Hart and Lady Jeanine walked over to Shawndra and looked at her intently. "She did get closer to the mists than any of us," said Hart.

"Yes," said the youthful Elder. "And I see a slight darkness over her that I have only seen from those who have tasted of the dark water."

Shawndra was confused by their words and was becoming more confused by the moment. She was having difficulty making sense of any thought. She was becoming anxious and fidgety for no real reason. There was a despair growing in her soul that she could not account for.

"We have little time," said Lady Jeanine. "I didn't expect to use this so soon." She took a small silver flask from her cloak and instructed Captain Hart to hold Shawndra in place. Hart took her arms, and Shawndra began to fight against him. The panic and fear of the dark water had begun to take her.

Lady Jeanine tilted Shawndra's head back and put one drop of clear water from the flask into the girl's mouth and then forced it shut. The Elder then began to sing a strange song.

Bah-rah-key nap-she et Mai, wuhall tish-kuh-chee kah-

all guh-moo-lah Has-so-lay-ahch luh-cahl chah woe nay key hah-rohphey luh-chahl-tah chahloo aychee Hago-ale mish-ah-chat chah-yehy chee hamuth chay tuh-ray chee hessed wuh-rah chameem. (103rd Song of Elders)

Almost immediately, Shawndra found herself calm again and stopped struggling against the Captain.

"What just happened?" asked Sebastian as he stood with his mouth open, watching all that had happened. The entire room was silent as Ba'ar, Bolo, and even Balam seemed to be intently watching what was happening.

"Are you well?" asked Jeanine to Shawndra. "Tell me of your thoughts."

"I'm confused. I don't understand what just happened," said Shawndra.

The Elder seemed to relax and stepped away from Shawndra. "You may let her go. She is capable of speech, and that is evidence enough that the sickness of the dead water has passed."

Captain Hart let her go and said, "Everyone pick up your gear, we need to keep moving." He returned to the place where he had put down his rucksack and started getting ready to move.

Shawndra said in a low voice to Lady Jeanine, "Really, please tell me what just happened." Shawndra was turning red and her eyes were watering. What she just experienced had scared her, as well as everyone else. She needed to make sense of it.

"My dear girl," said the Elder as she placed her

hand on Shawndra's cheek. "You ventured too close to the dark mists when we were outside and must have breathed some without even knowing it. The sickness that is caused by the dead water took a little longer to take effect, but no matter how much or how little you breathe, the effect is the same."

Shawndra had heard of what the dead water did to people, and she'd seen what it did to animals, but she never thought it would happen to her. "You mean I was going mad? I've heard of people that go crazy, or get sick and die because they are poisoned by the water." A new fear struck Shawndra. She realized that she had never heard of anyone coming back from the darkness, once it had begun. "Am I going to get sick and die?" Shawndra asked in a panic.

"No dear," said Jeanine with a smile. "The darkness has left you, and you are safe." Lady Jeanine held the silver flask in her hand so Shawndra could see and then returned it to her cloak.

"What did you give me? I've never heard of anyone recovering or being cured from the darkness." Shawndra was now more amazed than scared. The tears in her eyes were replaced with a sparkling excitement.

"I will tell you all in due time, but as you can see, it is time to push on." Lady Jeanine and Shawndra picked up their own rucksacks and the group gathered at the center of the rotunda.

Lady Jeanine stood with her back to the painting of the Elders laying the foundation to Falls Lake and raised her hand to signal for silence. "You have all been wondering how we will get past the falls. As you have seen through Shawndra's example, if we even get close to the mists, we will fall into the darkness of the dead water and may never return. So, the question is, how do we get over the falls when there is no path outside that is safe. The answer lies with you, Sebastian."

Everyone turned to look at Sebastian. Shawndra was puzzled, Bolo was smiling, Captain Hart was emotionless, and Ba'ar was annoyed, as usual. Sebastian wasn't sure what expression he had on his face, but he was sure he was not hiding his own confusion. "How do I have the answer?"

Lady Jeanine motioned for him to come forward. "Look on the painting behind me. Do you see anything familiar about it?"

Sebastian walked to the painting he had just passed moments earlier. He began to study it closer. There was a king and his son standing with the Elders. The stone they were laying had writing on it that Sebastian did not recognize. He saw the figure of Lady Jeanine in the form of an old woman. Sebastian thought that this was the most familiar form of the Elder that he knew. The young version that was with him now bore slight resemblances to the aged Elder that raised him. In the painting, she wore the traditional robes of the Elders. Sebastian saw something that made him move closer to the painting. One of Lady Jeanine's hands was holding something. It was a jeweled knife that had a very close resemblance to the one given him by the wild man. Sebastian placed his hand on the painting and realized that there was a hole where a jewel in the hilt of the small blade should be.

"I think I've found something," said Sebastian.

Sebastian didn't realize it, but no one had said a word while he studied the painting. Not even Ba'ar had spoken up or complained. Their gazes were fully fixed on Sebastian.

Lady Jeanine stepped forward and placed her hand caringly on Sebastian's shoulder, "I'd say that you have."

Sebastian continued, "There is a hole in the wall right where the dagger has been painted. Does that mean something?"

"Everything means something," replied the Elder.

Sebastian put down his rucksack and took out the jeweled knife. He began comparing it to the one in the painting. After studying and comparing them, he decided that they were indeed the same knife. He just didn't know what the significance was.

Lady Jeanine leaned over and whispered in Sebastian's ear, "Remember the words of the one who gave you that blade. He said, 'Carry these close to you, young Sebastian. They will help you find your path.'"

Sebastian thought, *If only I knew what he was talking about. The key to this whole thing must be on the dagger.* Sebastian's eyes grew wide as though he had just stumbled upon the answer. He grabbed the dagger by the hilt, drew it out revealing the shiny engraved blade and then thrust it into the hole in the wall. The odd notches on the hilt fit perfectly into the hole. Immediately there was a sound of popping and sliding that seemed to come from the other side of the great painting, and then a loud bang rang out. The painting began to move and slowly swung open.

Everyone, except the Elder, gasped at what they had just seen. Behind the painting was an entrance to a large tunnel. The torches that showed their way were newly lit and were gaining strength with every moment. Lady Jeanine took the first one out of its holder, turned to the others, and said, "Well done, Sebastian. Allow me to introduce you to the king's highway."

"What is the king's highway? And why is it behind a painting?" asked Bolo.

"This is the secret way that kings have taken out of the palace and beyond the great falls. Not even I may travel this path without the permission of the king," said Lady Jeanine.

"I thought you could go anywhere you wished," said Shawndra.

The Elder replied, "To travel this road you must have the proper key. The one that Sebastian so cleverly discovered."

"It wasn't that clever," mumbled Ba'ar. "I would like a closer look at that knife. In fact, should a simple boy like this even be allowed to keep such a blade? That seems to me an awful waste."

Sebastian sheathed the dagger and placed it back in his rucksack. "It was given to me for a reason. I think I'll hang on to it a little longer." Sebastian thought that if he were to give away his gift, he would give it to Bolo or Shawndra, but Ba'ar was the last person he would consider.

"Pick up your things," said Lady Jeanine. "Let's get moving again."

Sebastian swung his sack onto his back, and Jeanine led the way into the tunnel. It was big enough for everyone to walk through without having to hunch over or crowd each other. Even Balam with his packs had no trouble with the tunnel.

More paintings lined the walls. Most of them were stained with mold and time so that they were hardly recognizable. They seemed to be of events that Sebastian knew nothing of. He saw a painting of men dressed in black and carrying torches. They were with a soldier of the Citadel, and they were chasing someone from Falls Lake.

"Will you look at that!" said Bolo with surprise. "Is that who I think it is?" Everyone gathered round where Bolo was standing. Lady Jeanine brought her torch closer, and they all saw what made Bolo's jaw drop. In front of them was a painting of six travelers and a horse. There were two young people, three soldiers and an Elder with black flowing hair.

"Is that us?" gasped Shawndra.

"The king's highway was cut by Elders for the king. It goes into the mountain and therefore is the domain of the great Mai. I don't know who painted these walls, but these walls do tell a story," said Lady Jeanine.

"If they painted this in the past, and now we are seeing the present, maybe it will show our future," said Ba'ar. "We will know what we are to do next." Ba'ar took a torch off of the wall and began walking up and down the path trying to make sense of the other figures. There was a city in flames, a Baruk, and other things no one could make out. "How are we to go on if these walls don't tell us anything?"

"We don't need to know everything to know something Ba'ar," said Lady Jeanine. "The future is uncertain, and we have far to go. But we do know our next step."

"Oh yes, and what is that?" asked Ba'ar as he swung the torch toward Lady Jeanine.

"We must go to the end of this tunnel and get beyond the falls. And that is enough to know for now," said the Elder.

Ba'ar moved closer with his torch. It was now very close to the Elder's face. "And what if our ruin is out there? Did you think of that? What if there are bandits waiting for us at the end of the tunnel? What if there are giant leaches and other beasts that are going to snatch us up? I think we should study this wall and know what the future holds."

"Steady yourself, Ba'ar," said Captain Hart. "We are soldiers of the Citadel. Whatever is at the other end of this tunnel, we will face it." Ba'ar realized he had said too much and backed away from the Elder.

"The future is uncertain, that much is clear," said Lady Jeanine. "This painting tells us that Mai has ordered our steps, the great king under the mountain is with us. Since he has not seen to it to show us the details of our journey, then we can know that it is not for us to know at this time. So let us continue on."

Sebastian asked, "So, has our future already been written?"

"It has, but try as you will, you will not see it here," replied the Elder.

"How do we know we aren't headed for disaster?" Shawndra asked.

"I can assure you, we are. But *how* you face the challenge, the pain, the disaster, that is the true test," said Lady Jeanine.

"This Elder's mumbling is useless. If you know the rest of the story, then why don't you just tell us?" asked Ba'ar in a low voice, trying not to be corrected by Captain Hart again.

The Elder responded, "I am as much a part of the story as you. We all have our tests, and we all must face our fears. And right now our tests lie to the north."

Lady Jeanine turned and resumed her path. All of the group, even Ba'ar, followed after her. There were no more paintings that could be understood on the walls. Sebastian and Shawndra stayed close to each other on the steady incline of the path.

Sebastian heard a pebble roll behind them and turned but did not see anything. However, he got the distinct feeling that someone, or something, was following them. "Let's hurry up and get out of here. This place gives me the creeps." Sebastian sped up his pace and passed Bolo and Balam and walked closer to Captain Hart.

Lady Jeanine stopped at the end of the tunnel where a solid wall blocked their path. She called to Sebastian and said, "We need your key again."

Sebastian took out the dagger, found an opening and, like before, after a series of pops and grinds, the door slid open and the group walked out of the tunnel. It was midday now and the sun was high in the sky. They were standing on a path that led down to an ancient road. The roar of the falls was now behind them and Sebastian saw a large lake in front of them. The lake was dark and nothing grew on the banks. The bare rocks and sand did not add beauty to the poisoned water.

Lady Jeanine had put down her torch and continued on the narrow path. "We must go a little farther before we are able to stop. We need to get on the road that travels the edge of the lake. That will take us to the old ferry docks where we need to cross to the western side."

Once the group had cleared the tunnel and were almost to the road, Sebastian looked back at the entrance to the king's highway and was surprised to see the wild looking man standing at the entrance. He had been following them the entire time. The man then ran into the shrub trees that grew on the slope of the mountain and disappeared. Sebastian thought, *I knew someone was behind us.*

Just then, Sebastian heard Ba'ar's voice with its usual sarcasm, "Do try to keep up, little ones." Sebastian turned to see that the group had gotten far ahead of him.

He sprinted to Bolo and said, "I'll lead Balam for a while, you can take a rest from it."

Bolo smiled and said, "No rest is needed. This is a right smart beast. He goes when he's supposed to and stops before I even have to tell him. Yep, that's a right smart horse you got there." Balam whinnied and Bolo laughed. "Sometimes I think he knows what I'm sayin.'"

"He may, Bolo, he may at that," said Sebastian. The two and their horse brought up the rear of the group. Shawndra tried to walk with Lady Jeanine. Ba'ar and Captain Hart were in the middle. The group had already had a great adventure and the journey was just beginning.

SAVED BY SAP ROOT

"We're beginning to lose the light," said Ba'ar.

"I think he wants set up camp now," whispered Sebastian.

"I think he wanted to set up camp over two hours ago," whispered Shawndra.

Bolo chuckled as he led Balam up the path. Lady Jeanine had kept a brisk pace and had a campsite in mind. She passed up fair camping grounds twice before, and Ba'ar was faithful to let her know. Sebastian had not thought of Ba'ar as a whiner, but there he was, whining about the dreary day, the rocks, the water, the passing up of campsites.

Captain Hart had not uttered a word that was not militarily appropriate. He spoke mainly with Lady Jeanine and occasionally issued an order to Ba'ar or Bolo. Bolo didn't seem to mind. Sebastian knew this because Bolo would say, "I am just happy to be here."

Balam was also carrying his load without complaining. That is, complaining as far as horses go. Balam did not pull against the reins or didn't try to run off.

"What are those plants?" asked Shawndra.

"Bless me, I haven't seen those in years," said Bolo. They were walking past a patch of plants that looked like small round balls with prickly things all over them. At the top was a green stem with a flower. "Those are sap root plants."

Sebastian looked closer and said, "I've never heard of them."

"Oh, they're grand," said Bolo with a laugh. "Me and my paw-paw would grow these near the garden. The round part is full of sap, and the green stem on top is good and tough. It makes it easier to pull them out of the ground."

Shawndra cocked her head to the side and crinkled her nose and said, "What is so fun about pulling them out of the ground?"

Bolo laughed and said, "Pulling them out of the ground isn't the fun part. It's the lighting of the root and throwing it that is the fun part." His eyes shined with mischief. Bolo was still more of a boy than he was a man. He still enjoyed pranks and play. However, this masked a very keen mind.

Sebastian said, "Oh, I've heard of these after all. Farmer Levert once told me about boom root."

"Yeah, that's what I've heard other people call it," said Bolo.

Shawndra said, "I still don't understand the point of it all."

"There is no point," said Bolo as he laughed again.

"I sure would like to try out one of these plants," said Sebastian. "We could light one, and then we could put it in Ba'ar's rucksack." Both Bolo and Sebastian shared a devilish grin when Shawndra interrupted their wickedly fun fantasy.

"Don't you dare. I have no more love for that bully than anyone else, but any loud noises would give away our position. And I don't think Captain Hart would approve of that." Just the mere mention of Hart's name seemed to snap the two boys to attention.

"You're right," said Sebastian. And then he put his hand on Bolo's arm, "However, one day you'll have to teach me about how to use these plants."

Bolo's smile returned, and he said, "You've got it."

The three travelers doubled their pace to catch up with the rest of the group. They all passed over a sandbar that Sebastian figured had once been white. Now the dead water had stained everything a morbid grey and black color. Even the rocks were saturated with the haze of death. Lady Jeanine was mindful to stay clear of the water. Her eyes rarely looked away from it. Captain Hart, on the other hand, watched the woods. Between the vigilance of the two of them, Sebastian felt they were safe enough.

"That's where we should make camp tonight." Sebastian heard the youthful Elder's voice as she pointed to a high shelf of rock near the lake's edge. "We will be able to keep an eye on the tree line for a good distance, and it is defendable."

"I agree," said Hart. "This is good ground. Ba'ar, scout into the woods about half a hike and look for signs that people are near."

"Yes, Captain," said Ba'ar. He turned and walked back down the path where Sebastian, Shawndra, and Bolo were approaching and commanded Bolo to attention. "It's time for you to make yourself useful."

Bolo stood to attention as Ba'ar gave his orders. "The Captain has ordered you to scout into the woods about half a hike to find any signs of a threat. And while you're out there you are to gather some wood for a fire."

"And what will you be doing as Bolo does all the work?" asked Shawndra.

"I will be guarding the southern approach and securing our flank," said Ba'ar with a tone of importance. He then pushed past the three youngest of their group and their horse and walked back down the trail they had just traveled.

"I think, 'guard our flank' is code for take a rest," said Sebastian. All three of them smiled a knowing smile to each other.

"Rest or no rest, I've got my orders," said Bolo. "Here, you take the reins. That horse will just make noise and trample any signs I'm looking for that other people are near."

Shawndra said, "I'm going with you. I'll pick up fire wood and that will get us all back to the campsite sooner."

"And I'll take Balam and help set up camp," said

Sebastian. Balam whinnied as if he knew his heavy packs were coming off soon. The three of them separated, and Shawndra and Bolo disappeared into the thicket of trees as Sebastian led Balam to where Lady Jeanine and Captain Basher were standing.

The light was fading, and camp had not been properly set up. Sebastian began unloading their supplies from Balam. He was filling Balam's feed sack with grain when he heard a rustling from the bushes. The next thing he saw was a flash of steel and heard a scream of pain. Standing over him was Captain Hart with his sword drawn and bloodied. Lying on the ground, clutching his arm was a wild-eyed person that Sebastian had never seen. He had the look of death about him, and Sebastian knew that it was a man that had been driven mad by the dead water. He had sprung out of the bushes at Sebastian, and Captain Hart had moved quickly. Hart stood between Sebastian and the crazed person.

Sebastian looked frantically for Lady Jeanine and saw her in a crouching position with her sword drawn as well. "Get behind me, Sebastian," said the Elder.

The man holding his arm began screaming and babbling in a way that no one understood. He scrambled to his feet and ran back into the forest. "What was that?" asked Sebastian.

"Only a taste of what is to come, I fear," said Lady Jeanine as she stood up straight, refusing to sheath her sword. "I was hoping we would get farther north before we encountered them."

Ba'ar came running up the path and rejoined the group. "What did I miss?"

"You missed a mad man who tried to attack Sebastian," said Lady Jeanine.

"I told you to scout the woods. Why were you on the path south of us?" asked Hart as he sheathed his sword.

"Bolo insisted that he wanted to brush up on his tracking skills, so I let him scout the woods. And to be honest, he needs the practice." As Ba'ar said this he glared at Sebastian as a warning not to say anything to the contrary. "And that girl is with him."

"If there are more of these crazy people, shouldn't we go find Bolo and Shawndra?" asked Sebastian.

"No," said Hart. "That would just separate us and put us in the woods at dark making lots of noise and marking us as targets. They know where we are; we don't know where they are. We will stay here."

Sebastian put down his rucksack and pulled the jeweled dagger from it. "I guess I might need this," said Sebastian.

Captain Hart turned to him and said, "This man who attacked us, his clothes were stained and tattered, but I still recognized what he wore. He was a fisherman. He's been poisoned by the dead water, but he's no skilled warrior. I could have killed him, but I chose to wound him instead. If we can avoid taking a life, we must. So, put away your knife and pick up a handful of rocks, maybe even a sturdy stick. The people who have drank the dead water scare easily so if you hit them in the head with a rock or two, we may be able to run them off without badly hurting them." This was the first time Sebastian saw the Captain as compassionate or merciful. He was beginning to see that there was more to being a soldier than just swordplay and war.

In that instant a loud cry came up from the dark wood. Lady Jeanine turned and said, "How many do you reckon?"

Captain Hart said, "Sounds like at least twenty."

"Twenty? Do you mean people?" gasped Ba'ar.

Captain Hart glanced at Ba'ar and said, "Steady, soldier."

At the tree line, the shrubs began to shake and the noise of footsteps through dead underbrush could be heard. When the people emerged from hiding Sebastian could see that the Captain's estimate was very close. Sebastian counted a total of eighteen. They all shared the same expressions of the man who had just attacked them.

"We may not be able to hold them off without hurting them after all," said Hart. He was examining the group of hostiles slowly approaching them. They were snarling and growling like a pack of wild dogs circling their prey just before they strike.

"Should I use my dagger now?" said Sebastian as he was putting a couple of rocks in his pocket and picked up a sturdy stick.

"Get behind me!" said Lady Jeanine. "No matter what, don't let them put you in the water."

With a high-pitched scream that highlighted the insanity of the people, they all attacked. The space between the tree line and travelers from Falls Lake was covered swiftly. Even Hart seemed surprised at how quickly these people were able to cover the ground between them.

Just before the first person was able to attack, a sizzling streak of light passed in front of them and a loud thunderclap was heard. The would-be attackers halted their run in fear and began looking all around. Two more balls of light streaked in front of them, bounced on the ground, and then exploded with a deafening noise and bright light. Six of the crazed people were knocked backwards. With a cry of fear, they all began running for the safety of the forest as a tall, oddly shaped creature emerged from the southern path. It was able to throw fireballs from its hands and was covered in vines and leaves. The creature sent one more volley of exploding light behind them to encourage their flight.

The woods had quieted now that the last of the people infected with the darkness of the dead water had run away.

"What sort of creature is that?" said Ba'ar. "I don't know which is worse, a gang of crazy people or a beast that can throw fire from its hands." Ba'ar's sword was drawn, and his hands were shaking. He had never prepared to fight such a creature.

"Put away your weapon, Ba'ar," said Jeanine as she sheathed her own sword. "Nicely done, you two."

The creature replied with a voice that sounded very much like Bolo's. "Thank you kindly, my lady." As the vines and leaves fell to the ground, Sebastian was able to see that the terrible creature that had scared off their attackers was Bolo with Shawndra on his shoulders.

"Well done indeed," said Sebastian as he put his stick down and began emptying his pockets of rocks he had gathered to fling at anyone who tried to hurt him or his friends.

Shawndra climbed down from Bolo's neck and said, "We found the trail of those people when we doubled back and began to scout the woods."

"Yep," said Bolo. "I figure they've been following us for a couple of hours." He was still cleaning off the last of his disguise.

"How did you make fire balls come from your hands?" asked Sebastian.

"Me and Shawndra went to that sap root grove not too far back and gathered as many as we could carry. We thought they might come in handy," said Bolo as he smiled.

"Well done, Bolo," said Captain Hart. "You've always been keen on strategy. Today, if we only relied on the sword, we may have perished, but your bit of trickery was just what was needed. I can see now that you coming on this journey was a wise choice." Captain Hart winked at Bolo, who seemed more surprised at this compliment than at anything that had happened on this first amazing day.

"Well, to be honest, sir, Shawndra helped too." Bolo looked at his thirteen-year-old friend and smiled. "It was her idea to get on my shoulders and cover ourselves with vines so that we looked bigger than what we were."

Ba'ar seemed to have recovered himself and said, "Well, isn't that nice. Maybe the two of you can perform another amazing feat and set up camp and start a fire."

Sebastian wasn't sure if Ba'ar would have preferred being mauled to death by an angry mob rather than show Bolo and Shawndra some appreciation for saving his life.

"I think these two have earned some rest," said Lady Jeanine. "You two, go and unload the horse's supplies, and the rest of us will set up camp. And since you are so interested in having a fire, Ba'ar, you are in charge of collecting the firewood." Lady Jeanine turned away from Ba'ar and began unpacking her rucksack.

"Me, gather wood and—" said Ba'ar but was interrupted by a scathing look from Hart.

"We will all do our part, Ba'ar. Right now your part is gathering wood and starting a fire." Ba'ar felt shamed and skulked off to pick up whatever wood he could find.

Sebastian smiled at the thought of Bolo and Shawndra being honored and Ba'ar being sent off to pick up sticks. He thoroughly enjoyed the reversal.

After camp had been set up and a decent fire had

been started, Shawndra mixed a stew made from the dried meats and herbs she had brought from her parents. They were dipping their bread in it and drinking water, when Sebastian figured it was time he asked something that had been on his mind for quite a while.

"Lady Jeanine, what can you tell me about the dead water? Why does it affect people the way it does?"

Lady Jeanine put down her bread and answered, "There is no clear understanding of the dead water because only the living take the time and discipline to organize such thoughts. No, the dead things are stale and stagnant. The understanding of the dead water comes from tales and observations, but not personal experience. No one knows because you must have tasted the dead water to understand death fully. But once a person becomes dead, they are no longer interested in the living. So we will never have an exact understanding of the dead water. But it is sufficient to say that it is better to be alive than dead, and we will have to leave it at that."

"So how can we fight a thing, or even say a thing is bad, if we can't know all there is to know about it?" asked Ba'ar. These were the first words he had said since he had been sent to gather wood.

"You don't have to know everything in order to know something. Death isn't just about the dark water. There are other forms of death. Death is the product of treachery and foolishness. Death thrives in random anarchy at the whims of unrestrained passion. A numbness to the things of Mai and an apathy and resentfulness to all things living. A desire for all things to be as unhealthy as oneself so that self is the standard. The dead ones encourage death in others and will try to drag you to the place of dead water, throw you in, and try to make you drink."

From the top of the boulders on which they camped, Sebastian looked out over the lake that was poisoned by the black death. The wind came from the mountain and whipped through the trees and across the water and swirled around Sebastian. It brought with it a stench that seemed stronger here. Sebastian was shaken to the soul every time he thought about how close they were to oblivion. Walking on the path next to the lake was danger-ous, but it was the only path they could take. The towering granite mountains that reached to the sky on either side of the lake gave no inroads for men to follow. The sliver of land that could be traveled on foot between the grey foreboding walls of the mountain was all that was given to Sebastian and his group of friends to travel.

MEET the BARUK

The lady was up early. Something bothered her and kept her from resting during the night. She thought about the speed at which their enemies came upon them the day before, and she knew they didn't have any way to hold off a large number. Eventually the people sickened by the dead water would come back with a group so large that no amount of sap root plants would be able to save the travelers. The group needed more weapons and soldiers to fight a stronger enemy, and there simply weren't any more. "We need some help," said Lady Jeanine as she propped herself on her elbow looking into the cooling embers of what was left of the night's fire.

"What kind of help?" asked Sebastian as he sat up rubbing the sleep from his eyes.

"You are awake early. The sun has not yet shone itself over the mountains and you are stirring," said

Lady Jeanine. She sat up and moved closer to Sebastian offering him some water from a nearby skin.

"Thank you." Sebastian drank away the taste of sleep and then sat up straight. He looked at the auburn glow of the waning night's fire and said, "How many more of them are there?"

The Elder looked to the woods, "I don't know. I always hope for the best, but I also prepare for the worst. We need the kind of help that is fast and not afraid of battle." Jeanine stood up straight and resolute, looking to the east as if she already knew what must be done and where they had to go.

"There are only two options that we have, and one of them is impossible," said Captain Hart. He also had not slept well during the night. He kept one hand on his sword and both his eyes on the tree line the entire evening. "We can go back and bring more soldiers on horseback." Hart voiced this option in vain, he knew there was no turning back.

Bolo rolled over under a blanket that was too short and not wide enough to cover all of him at once. "I don't think we can use horses on this ground. The path is smooth enough for Balam, but we couldn't ride him into the forest where the rocks are sharp and jagged. Or is that the impossible option?" asked Bolo.

"No," said Hart. "The use of horses in a mountain range is nearly impossible. We can use them for packhorses and lead them with care, but to ride them swiftly to fight, they would break their legs and throw their riders. No, it is nearly impossible, but not as impossible as getting help from a Baruk."

Sebastian leaned forward with renewed interest in the conversation. "I've always wanted to see a Baruk." Sebastian was wide awake now with no hint of sleepiness. "Do they live near here?"

Lady Jeanine turned away from the east and looked to Sebastian and said, "No, they don't live near here, but they are always near." Sebastian never liked it when the Lady Jeanine was cryptic. But that was most of the time so Sebastian learned to read the silence.

"How do we find a Baruk?" asked Bolo.

Sebastian turned to Bolo with his eyes wide, "And once we find one, do we just ask it to help us? I mean, do they speak a different language?" Bolo shrugged, and they both turned to Lady Jeanine.

"While the Baruk don't live near here, they are always near. We must get to the east side of the lake. That is where we will have the best chance of making contact with them," said the Elder.

Captain Hart was adjusting his armor as he said, "The only place for that is the ferry at Carmel Point. But I don't even know if it is still there."

"If what is still there?" Shawndra had just woken up and was trying to catch up to the conversation. She looked blankly at Sebastian and then turned toward Hart who was finishing tightening his light armor and buckling his sword belt.

"The ferry is the only way to cross the lake from

the west side to the east side if you have a horse with you," said the captain as he drew his sword and inspected the blade closely.

"Why wouldn't it be there?" asked Sebastian.

Captain Hart said, "Neither myself nor Lady Jeanine have been upriver for over thirteen years. That's a long time for a boat to sit in the water. Especially when it's dead water."

Shawndra was wide awake now and leaned forward so close to the dwindling fire that the light from the coals danced on her face as she said, "What if something goes wrong with the ferry? What if it begins to sink? It's not like you can swim in the dead water. We all know what happens if you swallow any of that stuff. And I can't even take a bath without swallowing a few drops."

Ba'ar came up from near the woods where he had been keeping a watch for the past hour. He had a talent for hearing conversations from long distances, and he didn't hesitate to use the information against people. "If I'm not mistaken, I'd say you're afraid of the water."

"You would be a fool not to be afraid of the dead water," said Shawndra as she jumped to her feet, clenched her fists and glared at Ba'ar.

Ba'ar smiled wickedly he propped one foot on a rock and then leaned on his elbow, "That's just the sort of thing to hear from a little girl. I don't choose to make excuses for fear."

Lady Jeanine rolled up her blanket, secured it in a pack on the horse, and said, "A little fear would be wise, considering the consequences." She winked at Shawndra and then said, "Everyone get packed and ready to move. We will head upriver to the Carmel Ferry. The journey should take at least half a day, and there we will see if any of the boats can still be used. Pack up and leave as little evidence as possible that we were here."

———•———

The six companions and their horse had been walking together since the morning and the sun was climbing high into the noonday sky. Lady Jeanine was in the lead as usual and seemed to never tire. Behind her was captain Hart. Sebastian and Shawndra were walking side by side, after them was Bolo and Balam and Ba'ar bringing up the rear. Bolo was tiring and the horse was pulling him more than Bolo was pulling the horse. The ground was getting rockier, and the shoreline more steep.

They had all been walking since sunup, and after four hours with no break, some were showing signs of growing tired.

The western side of the lake wound around to the city of Sodorrah, and that was their destination. There they would resupply for their trip up the river of the dead water and find the source, and possibly put an end to whatever was feeding it poison. However, since they would probably not make it there if they remained on their present path, they would need to switch to the eastern shore. Once they reached the other side of the lake, they had another two-day journey to travel before they would be in sight of the fishermen's city.

Sebastian and Shawndra were talking as they went about what they would do if they were able to cleanse the spring and help bring new life into Crespin.

"I don't know exactly what I'll do, but I do know one thing, I don't think I want to work for Farmer Levert anymore," said Sebastian.

"I thought you liked working for old man Levert," said Shawndra. "He seems nice enough to me."

"Well yes, he's nice enough, but after seeing all of the things we've seen so far, I don't know how I could ever go back to being a shepherd. All I do is just sit around and watch the sheep," said Sebastian. "If Balam didn't come out every so often, I'd have no one to talk to." Sebastian turned and winked at the horse. Balam gave a nod that jerked Bolo's arm forward as he held onto the reins.

"Easy, fella. That arm is attached, and I want it to stay that way," said Bolo. "When we get all this dead water cleaned up, I'm gonna go swimming. I've heard lots of old folks tell me about swimming in the river and in the lake. I've always wanted to do that."

"Shawndra, what will you do once we've saved Crespin and all the people lavish you with gifts?" asked Sebastian.

Shawndra raised her chin and smiled because she knew exactly what she wanted. "I will join the Citadel and learn to be a soldier."

"Really, Shawndra, no kidding this time. What will you do when you get back?"

Shawndra turned with her mouth open and a surprised and hurt look on her face. "Sebastian, you know better than anyone else that that's my dream. I see them practicing all the time, and I can do all the things they do. I've whipped boys older and bigger than me, and I bet when I get older I can take on any man. How can you, of all people, not take me seriously?"

Sebastian was a little embarrassed and said, "I know it's your dream and all, but there has never been a girl soldier in Crespin, and I just don't want you to get your hopes up."

"Well, look at Lady Jeanine," said Shawndra pointing ahead as they could see the Elder leading the way on the trail with a sword at her side, standing tall and strong. "You don't question whether or not Lady Jeanine should lead us on the trail or go with us into danger. You don't doubt her just because she's a woman."

"That's different," said Sebastian. "She's an Elder. Elders have been trained to lead their whole lives. No one truely knows their power or strength, except for other Elders. But you, you're just a girl."

Those last words stung Shawndra in a very personal way. She was torn between the impulse to run into the woods and cry or to turn and punch Sebastian in the nose. Instead she did nothing and walked the rest of the way in smoldering silence.

"We'll stop here to eat and rest," said Lady Jeanine. They had come to a clearing next to the mirky water with flat stones where they could build a fire. The woods were dense but open enough to walk through. Everyone placed their burdens on the ground, and Bolo led the young horse into the clearing and poured out some water and put some oats out for him to eat.

Captain Hart stood looking into the woods and had his hand on the hilt of his sword. "What do you see, Captain?" asked Jeanine.

"I feel that unfriendly eyes are on us. I've felt it for the last half hour." With a motion of his hands to Ba'ar and Bolo, the three soldiers took defensive positions around the rocks. "I don't know what's out there or whether it will give us any trouble, but it is best if we are prepared. Sebastian, you and Shawndra and Lady Jeanine eat and the rest, we three will eat where we are." As Captain Hart said this, he reached into his pack and pulled out a small cake of grains and berries. That, along with a cut of dried beef and a few swallows of water would be enough to keep him going for a while.

"I don't see Shawndra," said Sebastian. "I don't see her anywhere. She must have walked into the woods just as we began to put our packs down." Sebastian was getting frantic because of the warnings from Captain Hart.

"Sebastian, why would Shawndra go into the

woods on her own?" asked Lady Jeanine. "What would make her leave the safety of the group?"

Sebastian flushed at the idea that his careless words may have caused his friend to leave. "I told her that it was silly to wish to be a soldier of the Citadel, and that she couldn't do it because she was only a girl." Sebastian felt awful, not that what he believed he said was wrong, but because he had upset his friend and she may have run into danger.

"That's the only thing you've said that I agree with since we've started this journey," said Ba'ar. "Women don't belong at the Citadel. Men are soldiers and women are—" just then he realized that Lady Jeanine was staring at him anticipating his answer. "Well, men are soldiers, and that's all there is to say on the matter." Ba'ar turned to Captain Hart and stood straight and said, "Permission to go after the little runt and bring her back, Captain."

"Yes, Ba'ar, go and find her. Bring her back safely," said the Captain. "But, be careful, I still suspect that something is out there."

"I'll be back in a few minutes. Besides, how far could one little girl have gotten?" asked Ba'ar as he turned and weaved his way through the trees and under-brush. Soon he was out of sight, and the remainder of the group took the opportunity to rest and eat.

———

Shawndra was walking through the woods keeping careful note of where she was so that she wouldn't get lost. She felt that she had to step away for a few minutes in order to keep from seriously harming Sebastian. It was for his own safety that she took this little walk. She could hear the wind rustling the leaves and causing the trees to sway back and forth. Her eyes were on the ground, and she was breathing heavily, trying to calm herself.

"Just a girl, just a girl indeed. He didn't say that the time I pulled another boy off him. He didn't say that when I was chosen by Lady Jeanine to go with them. Ooh, I should have popped him when I had the chance," Shawndra mumbled to herself. It was that moment when she heard a noise in the leaves that sounded like soft footsteps. She looked up expecting to see someone from her party coming to fetch her, as if she was too small and too girlish to walk by herself. When she raised her head, she found herself looking straight into the eyes of a giant beast. The deep black eyes were set forward with an intensity she had never seen before. This creature looked like a wolf, only much, much larger. The hairs on the back of its giant neck were bristled and its teeth protruded over its gums revealing the deadly weapons in its mouth.

Shawndra stumbled backward and fell down, allowing her to get a much better look at the creature. She had heard of the giant creatures called Baruk. They walked on all four legs and the height of their backs was taller than a full-grown man. The Baruk were capable of running as fast as a horse and of climbing as well as a mountain goat. This creature's muscular shoulders and neck gave some indication of his power. This Baruk's feet were adorned with long sharp claws.

"You shouldn't be here!" came the low growl of the Baruk.

"You can speak?" said Shawndra. Her own ability to ask a question at a time like this surprised even her.

"Go back to your group; you are not safe here. Go now!" The Baruk sent a ripple through his body that showed a glimpse of his strength. The forcefulness of his words told Shawndra that she should do exactly as he said.

Shawndra scrambled to her feet and ran as fast as she could to get back to where the rest of her friends were. She didn't care now about having her feelings hurt; she would just have to punch Sebastian in the nose later. For now, Shawndra wanted to get back to the rest of the group in one piece.

"There you are! You shouldn't be out here by yourself," said Ba'ar as he saw her come over the top of a small hill.

Shawndra ran right past him and said, "Quick, run!" Shawndra didn't slow down for a moment as she ran past Ba'ar.

Ba'ar laughed as he watched her run. "Silly little girl, probably saw a lizard or a mouse." Ba'ar turned to look in the direction Shawndra came from and standing on top of the hill was the Baruk. He growled and showed his teeth and bristled the fur on his back.

Ba'ar turned and ran as fast as he could and passed Shawndra just before they cleared the tree line.

Ba'ar burst through the trees ahead of Shawndra and was having difficulty forming words between gulps of air. "It's a big...thing...with huge teeth.... and furry!"

Shawndra said, "I think it's a Baruk. It looks like a giant wolf, and it spoke to me!"

Ba'ar looked at her with a scowl and said, "It was a giant boar or a bear; Baruk are just legends. Old wives' tales that little girls enjoy talking about." Ba'ar turned to Captain Hart, "I'm not sure what it was, but it was large and dangerous."

"Is that what caused you to run past the person I sent you to protect, Ba'ar?" said the Captain.

Ba'ar then realized that in his effort to get away from what he thought was a giant beast, he had completely forgotten about Shawndra, and had even run past her to get away from danger. Ba'ar felt embarrassed, not because he had risked some- one else's life to protect his own, but because he had done it in front of the Captain.

"It was a Baruk," said Lady Jeanine. "He's been following us all day. However, that is not what the Captain has been sensing this half hour."

"What are Baruk?" asked Bolo.

"Baruk are creatures, like wolves but intelligent. Before men lived in the land of Crespin, the Baruk wandered the mountains. They sought out the source of the living spring and drank from it and were given the gift of intelligence. They were able to communicate with many creatures and can talk to men. They prefer to live in the rugged mountains where they are undisturbed."

"That is something you should have told us before we set out on this journey. We could have brought spears to use to defend ourselves," said Ba'ar with an aggravated tone.

"You need not fear the Baruk, their hearts are true. If it were not so, then the living water would not have given them the ability to speak. Besides, you would need ten men with spears to stop a Baruk. And even then, I doubt that you would live through it. No, there are other things in the woods that are much more worthy of our attention."

"More worthy than a seven-foot monster? What could possibly..." At that moment, a horn was blown from inside the woods and the cries of crazed men could be heard. Captain Hart drew his sword and his dagger, and Ba'ar and Bolo did the same. Shawndra picked up a rock, and Sebastian drew his dagger. Lady Jeanine stood straight and calm as the sound of approaching danger was heard. The wild screams and heavy footsteps of running men could be heard and then they saw the silhouette deep in the woods of many men coming at them. They were all carrying clubs and rocks and odd shaped things that they picked up off the ground. Any soldier could defeat one of them, possibly even two. But it was three soldiers, one Elder, and two children against thirty men.

Captain Hart commanded Ba'ar and Bolo, "Don't let anyone through and don't let them push you into the water."

"Yes sir," said Bolo as he held his sword in a defensive position.

At that moment, a loud howl rang out, and all the men that were attacking stopped immediately. Out of the forest lunged the giant Baruk. He leaped into the space between the crazed men and their supposed victims. A deep and terrible sound came from the Baruk as he faced the attackers and said, "If you wish to harm them, you must go through me, and I will cut you to pieces!" He then let out a loud and fierce noise that shook the ground, and the men turned in panic and ran back into the woods.

After the last man had passed out of sight, the Baruk turned and walked to the group. Captain Hart, Ba'ar, and Bolo still had their swords drawn, and Ba'ar wished he were still facing thirty men rather than this large creature. Jeanine stepped out between Hart and Ba'ar and approached the Baruk. The Baruk bowed by lowering his head and curling one leg underneath him.

"I have come to honor the last of the Elders," spoke the Baruk.

"I am Lady Jeanine, last of the Elders, you honor me." She placed her hand on the soft fur on top of the large Baruk's head. "What do they call you, noble creature?"

"I am Skiatook, in the tongue of man. I am the son of Kronos. I am here to escort you on a safer path than the one you have chosen." Skiatook was no longer bowing but standing on all fours looking intently over the motley party. "Why have you brought children on such a perilous journey?"

"Their presence is required," said Lady Jeanine. "They will prove themselves to be true. Are you going to take us by way of your home?"

"No!" said Skiatook as he instinctively bristled at the idea. "It is forbidden for outsiders to pass through our home. Only those who are proven worthy may enter. If it were you alone, Elder, then you could pass through, but none of these can be trusted."

"Not even this one?" said Jeanine as she turned and gestured to Sebastian.

"What is so special about that one?" asked Skiatook.

"Come see for yourself."

Skiatook walked past Captain Hart and Ba'ar, and his size pushed them apart. Skiatook stood over Sebastian as Lady Jeanine said, "Don't worry Sebastian, just be still."

"I'm not worried, my lady," said Sebastian. Skiatook smelled the air around Sebastian and said, "He speaks the truth; he is not worried. But is he afraid?" Skiatook asked as he looked down on Sebastian.

"I am afraid, a little," said Sebastian. "But I won't run."

"Brave lad," said Skiatook. "Only a fool would not be afraid of a Baruk the first time he saw one. However, only a wise man worthy of trust would admit the fear. You will grow stronger as you are able to face your fears."

"Is that all you can tell about him?" asked Jeanine. "Look deeper, Skiatook, look for something familiar." Skiatook looked puzzled at the words of the Elder, but he did as she requested. Skiatook drew a deeper breath and closed his eyes and held the smells in his sensitive nostrils for a moment to search every smell, every memory, and then his eyes opened and he said, "There it is," he said in a voice so low it was barely audible. Skiatook looked down at Sebastian and asked, "Who is your father?"

Sebastian was startled at such a question. So much of his past and his father was shrouded in mystery and this clue was even more mysterious than any other. "I'm sorry but, I don't know how my father has anything to do with this."

"If your father is who I think he is, it has every-thing to do with this," said Skiatook.

"You can answer him, Sebastian, go ahead," encour-aged Lady Jeanine who was now sitting on a stone and eating some food she had kept in her rucksack.

"My father is Cakal Corvin. He disappeared many years ago, on the day of my birth," said Sebastian.

"Your father is Corvin? While he is known to you

by that name, he is known to us as Nabok, blood brother to Kronos, my father. That makes you and I brothers, young Sebastian." Sebastian was startled at that revelation. How could he be brother with a Baruk?

"I can see you have many questions. They all must be asked, and Kronos himself will decide if they will be answered. But as for now, eat what you need to continue. We must make it to the ferry. Those men infected with the dead water will return. Their numbers will be larger, and I believe they will not be turned so easily."

"I thought you said that outsiders were not allowed to enter your home?" asked Captain Hart.

"No," said Skiatook as he turned his massive gaze to the Captain. "I said that outsiders that had not been proven could not pass through my home. Young Sebastian's father has guaranteed Sebastian's entry. The Elder is permitted, but the rest of you will have to be tested."

"And just what is this test?" asked Bolo as he stepped forward.

"Don't worry, you will see. As for now, eat quickly and regain your strength. We will need to leave soon because the men who have been driven mad by the dead water will return.

"Are there any more of you?" asked Captain Hart as he sheathed his sword and returned his dagger to its scabbard.

Skiatook lifted his great head and gazed across at the eastern shore. "We don't live on the western shore. I was sent to see to it that you made it to the ferry. There will be more of us once we cross over. My brother Verdigris will be one of the Baruk that will welcome us. You will know him by his grey fur and green eyes. He is the only one among us with such coloring."

Bolo and Ba'ar followed their captain's example and put away their weapons. Bolo quickly began to scurry around, picking up whatever had fallen or had been placed on the ground and then began to store in the packs on Balam. Balam, in the midst of all of this, had also stood his ground. Any other unremarkable animal would have run off or caused a commotion in panic. But Balam did as he was supposed to. Once everything was gathered and every person had a handful of food to eat on the way, they continued their journey, except now they were being escorted by the magnificent Skiatook of the Baruk.

The journey to the ferry only took a few hours. Everyone's pace was quickened since Skiatook was encouraging them to move faster. Skiatook had little patience with anyone other than Lady Jeanine and Sebastian. He answered the captain's questions with a slight tone of annoyance. But that was better than how he completely ignored Ba'ar. Bolo was too amazed to ask any questions, and he and Shawndra just walked behind the Baruk and marveled at the sight.

When they had all arrived at the ferry crossing, they saw the stone foundation with the burned out remains of an old building. Skiatook looked back and said, "This is where the ferry landed on the western side of the lake so many years ago." Skiatook then picked up his walk to a trot and moved quickly to a stone pier that was built over the water. There everyone saw a large ferry tied up to one of the posts.

Bolo's face lit up, "Lucky for us what ever happened to that old building didn't happen to the boat."

Lady Jeanine spoke with a look of great concern on her face, "There were once four ferry boats, and I think over there are the remains of the other three." The lady pointed to the far side of the old stone foundation where everyone could see the remains of three burned out boats. The ferry boat was built like a pontoon. It had two large timbers at least three feet thick from the base of a tree on either side. Several smaller poles crisscrossed between them to support the deck that was made up of flat boards. Two large oars, one on each side, and a rudder at the back powered the flat boat. All that was left of the fleet of ferries was the burned out remains of three on the shore and one very questionable boat in the water.

"How did this boat survive while the others were burned?" asked Shawndra.

Ba'ar replied, "Obviously because it was in the water. You can't burn wet wood. Honestly, you ask the most ridiculously obvious questions." Ba'ar turned away from Shawndra and met the gaze of Skiatook.

"The question is a worthy one. And the answer is not as obvious as you have assumed." Skiatook turned and began walking down to the dock. "Before the dead water came, this ferry was the only way for people on the western and eastern shores to trade without having to travel for days by foot around the lake. If you walked by way of Sodorrah, you would have to pay a tax. If you went to the south, by way of Falls Lake, it could take days. This way people could cross the lake in a matter of hours. When the dead water came, all four of the boats were moored on the western side here. As the people became infected with the dead water and the darkness entered their souls, they burned the boats and that building and tried to kill the ferry owner and his family. However, he took his family, and whoever was left that was not poisoned by the water, and they took the last ferry to the eastern side."

"So this ferry has been on the eastern side of the lake for thirteen years? How has the dead water not rotted it to the point that it is no longer useful?" asked Captain Hart.

Skiatook answered, "Kronos was told by the one with the fallen crown that the ferry must be saved. I was sent with my brother Verdigris to drag the ferry from the water high onto the bank so it could be used on the day that was appointed."

As everyone walked across the pier to the ferry, they got a good look at the boat in which they would trust their lives.

"It has holes in the deck," said Ba'ar. "This thing will never make it across the water."

"Have some courage, trembling one," said Skiatook with what Sebastian thought was a hint of sarcasm. "I brought the ferry over from the eastern shore and I tested every board. I put the holes in the deck so no one would put any trust in a rotten board. If you don't step in a hole, you won't fall through the deck."

Ba'ar flushed red with anger. He would have screamed insults at the Baruk had he not thought that the huge creature might take his head off for it.

"I have some questions," said Shawndra. "Who is the…" Shawndra never got to finish her question when they heard the familiar terrifying sound of trumpets and angry shouts from behind them.

"Quickly, we have little time," said Lady Jeanine. She drew her sword and slashed the ropes that secured the ferry to the pier. "Everyone get on the ferry now!"

Skiatook stayed on the pier while Captain Hart, Ba'ar, Sebastian, and Shawndra jumped across to the ferry. Bolo took Balam's reins and led him to the edge of the pier. "You'll have to make a bit of a jump little friend," said Bolo to Balam.

"Are you mad?" asked Ba'ar. "Leave that horse here and just take the packs. This ferry can't take that kind of weight."

Bolo looked at him unbelievingly and said, "If we leave him here there's no knowing what they'll do to him. And he's a right smart pony. He'll be fine."

Ba'ar snapped, "That's enough! I've had it with you. You and all these other children that just don't know anything about anything. That horse won't even be able to get on the barge much less…"

At that moment, Sebastian whistled and Balam leaped across to the ferry, almost knocking Ba'ar to the deck.

Shawndra walked over to Ba'ar who was still on the ground and said, "Skiatook already said the deck was solid. And I bet he weighs more than that horse." Hart jumped across to the ferry and was followed by Lady Jeanine.

Captain Hart had found the oars and tossed one on the ground next to Ba'ar. "Get up, and start rowing. You can help him, Bolo." Both young men used the oars to push the ferry away from the pier and then plunged the paddle deep into the murky water and began to row.

Lady Jeanine took hold of the rudder and shouted, "We must paddle fast, but don't splash any of the dead water. If any gets on you or in you it can be deadly."

Sebastian and Shawndra were convincing Balam to lay down at the front of the ferry. Balam went to his knees and finally settled himself on the deck. Skiatook was still on the pier as Captain Hart on one side and Bolo and Ba'ar on the other rowed hard to safety.

Skiatook looked back and shouted, "I'll stay here and make sure this mob doesn't reach the end of the pier until you are clear."

Lady Jeanine called back, "How many of them are there?

"I would say double what attacked you earlier

today." Skiatook let out a terrifying howl and showed his teeth but the crazed mob paid no attention. They still rushed at him holding sticks and rocks.

As the ferry cleared the end of the pier Lady Jeanine called out, "Now Skiatook!"

The great Baruk turned and with a few powerful strides leaped off the end of the pier. As he landed on the back of the ferry it gave them enough of a push to get them a safe distance from the crazed people that were trying to hurt them. A few of the people tried to catch them by leaping off the pier themselves. But they didn't have the strength of a Baruk. As Captain Hart and his two young soldiers continued to row and Lady Jeanine steered the ferry, Sebastian and Shawndra breathed a little easier. They could see the crazed shouting people on the shore getting smaller and smaller. They set their eyes to the eastern shore and took confidence that for the moment, they were safe.

THE TEST

The sound of oars pushing the ferry forward and the grunts of those rowing was all that was heard from the small group. Skiatook had settled on the back of the boat in order to counter balance the weight of the horse on the front of the boat. He sat in front of Lady Jeanine who was holding the rudder, and the two of them whispered to each other, but no one could hear what they were saying. Bolo and Ba'ar were getting winded from rowing, but to no surprise at all, Captain Hart worked silently and showed no sign of tiring.

Finally, Shawndra broke the silence. Her curiosity was bursting and some things that Skiatook had said only prodded her mind to ask more questions. "Mr. Skiatook. What did you mean by—" Shawndra was interrupted.

"I am no mister!" Skiatook almost spat the words out. "To be a mister, I would have to be a man. I am a Baruk. And I am only Skiatook."

"Oh, sorry," said Shawndra. She did not understand the offense taken by Skiatook. She only knew that none was meant. "You mentioned that a man with a *fallen crown* told you to save the ferry?"

Skiatook rested his head on his giant paws that were crossed in front of him. "Rest your mind, young one. If you are allowed to travel to the home of the Baruk then you may ask Kronos. Until then, I will answer no more questions."

Shawndra turned with a huff and leaned against Balam. Lady Jeanine spoke up, "We will reach the eastern shore in just a few moments. Jump to the rocks and make sure you don't get into the dead water."

Sebastian looked forward and saw the boulders and rocks that they were approaching. They looked as if they had been tears shed by the granite mountains behind them. The eastern shore was the same as the western shore with a narrow strip of beach between the water and the woods. However, the eastern shore had more trees and less rocky ground on which to travel. Sebastian thought it was unfortunate that they could not have traveled on this side of the lake to begin with. But every crossing from Falls Lake was dangerously close to the deadly mists churned up by the great water fall of dead water. They had to travel the western shore. Sebastian felt a glimmer of hope that things were about to get easier on this side of the lake.

Lady Jeanine called out to them and said, "Get ready up there. We will be close to that big boulder with the flat top. Sebastian, you go first and get Balam to follow you. Then Shawndra, and the rest of us will follow."

Sebastian and Shawndra stood up and coaxed Balam into standing. The young horse was unsteady on the moving boat, but he did not panic.

"Steady now, get ready," called Lady Jeanine. "Now, Sebastian!" Sebastian jumped from the deck of the ferry and landed on the flat top of the boulder. He turned and whistled for Balam, but the horse had already followed his example and jumped over and was standing over him.

"Wow, you did that all on your own, boy. That's great." Sebastian stroked the nose of his horse.

"Not as great as you moving your horse to the beach so we can all jump off," yelled Shawndra, who was waiting to jump over to the rock herself. Sebastian led Balam down the natural stairway of boulders to the beach that had very coarse sand and was stained a grey black color due to the dead water. Shawndra jumped clear and then Bolo, Ba'ar, and Captain Hart.

Skiatook stood to his feet and began talking to Lady Jeanine, "I'll go next and prepare the way for..." Before Skiatook could finish two men jumped from the water behind the boat and grabbed the Elder's legs and pulled them out from under her. She was taken by surprise and didn't even have time to grab on to anything as she was dragged into the dead water. The men had been in the water and holding on to the underside of the ferry boat all the way across the lake. No one had even suspected that they were there. The dead water had even covered their scent from the Baruk. As soon as the boat reached shallow water and they could get some footing, they jumped up and grabbed the feet of the only person they could reach. As Lady Jeanine was dragged into the water, she reached up to the sky in sheer desperation and her arm was caught in the mouth of Skiatook. The Elder was covered up to her neck by dead water. With a single motion he had pulled her out of the water so hard she flew through the air and landed on the beach in front of the boat, rolled over a couple of times and laid motionless. The two crazed men tried to jump out of the water and attack Skiatook but with one swipe of his great paw, he dispatched both of them with the cruelest efficiency.

Sebastian cried out, "My lady!" as he dropped Balam's reins and ran to the Elder. She was crumpled into a ball on the beach, and as Sebastian knelt by her side he saw streaks of gray where once only dark youthful hair had been. Sebastian put his hand on Jeanine's shoulder and pulled her back to lay on his lap, and he gasped as he saw a much aged woman laying there. She opened her eyes to reveal that they were no long as bright and alive as Sebastian had come to expect. They seemed cloudy and dull. The veins in her neck were growing black against her pale skin; she had been poisoned by the toxic water. Sebastian's hands began to burn, and he realized that Lady Jeanine was soaked in dead water.

Sebastian felt a thud in the earth and looked up and the mighty Baruk had jumped clear of the ferry and landed on the beach near him. "Wrap her in her blanket and then place her at the tree line where the woods meets the beach."

Sebastian could feel the tears gathering in his eyes as he realized that dead water didn't just make the Elder sick, it was possibly the only thing that could kill her. "We need to help her. What can we do?"

"I've told you what to do, little brother." Skiatook's words were calm, even caring. "Wrap her in her blanket and carry her to the edge of the woods. I know what to do."

Bolo had heard the request and pulled the Elder's blanket that she used for sleeping at night from the packs that Balam carried. Shawndra, Ba'ar, and even Captain Hart all stood helpless behind Sebastian, watching in vain.

Captain Hart asked, "What can we do?"

Skiatook answered, "I will take the Elder to my home where we can treat her. You will lead your group and your horse deep into the forest and to the base of the mountain. There you will find a path that leads north. Follow that path until one of my kind come for you."

After Sebastian and Shawndra had finished wrapping the Elder in her blanket, Captain Hart picked her up and carried her to the wood's edge. The Elder's skin was growing pale and where once a young powerful woman had been, a frail aged Elder had taken her place. The power that changed Lady Jeanine to the image of her youth had been undone by the dead water.

Skiatook said, "I haven't much time." He scooped Lady Jeanine into his great jaws and picked her up and leaped into the dark woods. He wasn't trying to be stealthy as he ran and the sound of his great weight crashing through the woods could still be heard long after he had disappeared from sight.

Sebastian stood for a moment in silence as his gaze lingered on the spot where Skiatook and the Elder had disappeared into the darkness. A single tear threatened to fall as he remembered the words she had repeated to him since he was a child. "We must trust in the will of Mai."

Sebastian turned from the woods and ran to the shoreline. There he picked up his rucksack that he had thrown off to help his friend the Elder. The wide-eyed look of a boy was gone from his face and the resolute look of a young man had replaced it. "We know what to do," he said. "We will travel to the base of the mountain and then head north."

No one questioned or even hesitated what Sebastian had said. Even Ba'ar picked up his rucksack without complaint. Bolo took Balam's reins, and with Captain Hart in the lead, they all set off to continue the journey.

The five from Falls Lake and their horse traveled without their new guide, Skiatook, and the Elder for many hours. Sebastian and Shawndra had become exhausted because they were all trekking up hill into the rocky mountains that border the northeastern part of Crespin. Somewhere in these mountains, shrouded in secrecy, was the home of the Baruk. The events of the day had tired out every member of the small group, especially Sebastian and Shawndra, and their legs were becoming wobbly and unstable. Shawndra, who was usually defiant to any help offered her because she thought it would make her seem more like a little girl, was now clinging to the side of Balam's packs, relying on the young horse to pull her up hill.

The group had reached the path that followed the base of the mountain, and the trail was easier to follow. The sun was setting behind the mountain, and everyone's mind turned toward making camp. However, Captain Hart had not slowed or made any mention of looking for a suitable place to bed down for the night. He remained at the lead point, looking intently at every rock and tree that they had passed. He was reading the signs around him, and something told Sebastian that he didn't like what they said.

"Everyone stop," said Hart. He drew his sword and dagger, and Bolo and Ba'ar copied his every move. Sebastian drew his gold jeweled dagger, and Shawndra picked up a rock. Then Captain Hart did something very unexpected. He dropped both his sword and dagger on the ground and raised both arms. Sebastian looked at Ba'ar and saw that his mouth was wide open with astonishment. He then looked at Bolo and saw that he had done the same thing. Captain Hart turned and with a stern look to Ba'ar told him to drop his weapons and do the same. The loud clank of cold steel as it hit the rocks on the path echoed off the great granite slope of the mountain. Sebastian also dropped his dagger, and the sound of Shawndra dropping her rock was the last sound the small group made.

"That was very wise of you humans. Very wise indeed." The voice was not entirely familiar, but also not entirely foreign. The hulking mass of a Baruk came from behind a large boulder ahead of the travelers. He did not have the dark features of Skiatook, this was a different Baruk. He had grey fur and the deepest green eyes anyone could imagine. Sebastian knew immediately who he was.

"You are Verdigris, brother to Skiatook and son of Kronos," said Sebastian.

"And you have the training of an Elder about you," said the Baruk. "You must be the one Skiatook told me about." As with Skiatook, the Baruk walked past everyone else and faced Sebastian. He breathed deeply the air about him and closed his eyes. When he opened them again he laughed aloud and said, "I am indeed Verdigris of the Baruk. And you are Sebastian of the man tribe. I am told that you are my little brother."

"Yes," said Sebastian. "I've been told the same thing."

The Baruk turned and began to walk swiftly up

the path and called back, "The sky is growing dark, and we have little time. Make haste, humans."

Captain Hart quickly picked up his weapons and sheathed them. Ba'ar and Bolo did the same, and Sebastian picked up his dagger. Ba'ar looked over at Shawndra and said with a sneer, "Aren't you going to pick up your rock?"

Shawndra said, "There are rocks aplenty here. But I'll be looking for one with your name on it." Ba'ar turned in a huff and began running down the path to catch up with the Baruk.

Everyone had to run just to keep sight of Verdigris. The Baruk seemed to be in a great hurry, and he didn't seem to care that every member of the group that was following him was ready to collapse from exhaustion. After Sebastian and Shawndra had fallen their own fair share of times, Verdigris stopped and said, "Bring my little brother to me, as well as the girl." Bolo turned and helped Sebastian and Shawndra up the path to where Verdigris was waiting. "Now, help them onto my back. I will carry them the rest of the way."

Verdigris lowered himself close to the ground, and Bolo helped lift Sebastian and Shawndra onto Verdigris' back. Shawndra let out a weak protest, saying something about how she could continue on foot, but Bolo noticed that she didn't protest too much. Once on his back, the two held onto his thick fur as Verdigris raised up and resumed his course along the path.

Bolo turned to Captain Hart and said in astonishment, "I've never heard of anyone riding a Baruk before. I didn't know it was possible."

"From what I've heard it's only by invitation. If anyone tried such a foolhardy thing without a Baruk's permission, they will find themselves missing an arm or some more vital part of their body," said Captain Hart.

"Wow, how heavy a load can one of those creatures carry up a mountain?" asked Bolo.

"They can carry a full grown antelope in their mouths or a full grown man on their backs without much trouble," said the Captain.

"If we're not careful, he may carry a full grown man in his mouth to this people," said Ba'ar in a low tone.

"If Skiatook wanted us dead, we would be dead. Besides, they like the taste of wild game, they have no liking of humans as food," said Hart.

"Still, I don't trust them. We should have brought spears," said Ba'ar.

"That's enough. Verdigris has not threatened us. We will trust him for as long as he shows himself to be trustworthy," said Captain Hart. "Now, let's get back to following before Verdigris gets too far ahead and we lose sight of him. Bolo, how is the horse doing?"

Bolo had began checking Balam's hooves while Ba'ar was talking. "He's fine, sir. He's a right strong little horse. He hasn't stumbled once. However, I don't know how much farther we can take him because this trail is turning into a mountain, and Balam here isn't as good a climber as that Baruk."

"We will deal with that when the time comes. Let's bring him as far as we can take him," said Captain Hart. Captain Hart lead his men down the path, following after Verdigris and the children.

They finally reached a point at which Verdigris came to a stop and turned and faced everyone. The stone wall around him seemed to have deep gouges as if something had been trying to climb the mountain from here. He lowered himself to the ground, and Sebastian and Shawndra slid off his back and went to stand with Captain Hart and the rest of the group. Verdigris spoke, "This is where some of you will continue with me, and some of you will continue on the path alone. You must take a test, and if you speak the words of truth, you will pass and will sleep in the home of the Baruk tonight. However, if you fail, you will stay at the base of the mountain."

"What sort of test is that?" asked Ba'ar. "What do you mean, words of truth? Why not test our strength or our skill? Who has ever heard of such a test?"

"You wish to enter my home, so the test is of my making," said Verdigris with a low growl.

"I am ready to take your test," said Sebastian as he stepped forward to stand directly in front of Verdigris. "What do I have to do?"

"You don't have to take this test, little brother. Your father's actions in the past have shown your blood to be worthy of trust," said Verdigris. "You are one of the Baruk, and always welcome in our home."

"I want to take the test. I never knew my father and to be judged poorly or fairly by his actions is unfair. Please, put me to the test and allow me to earn your trust," said Sebastian.

Verdigris raised his head and gave out what seemed to be a laugh. Sebastian wasn't even sure if these creatures could laugh. "You are indeed the son of Corvin, and you have passed the test. Tonight you will know the hospitality of the Baruk."

"I don't understand," said Shawndra. "You didn't ask him anything. How could he pass a test of truth?"

Verdigris replied, "The test is not a test of knowledge, but of how willing you are to speak the truth. Sebastian wanted to prove his worthiness and said so. He told the truth about how he felt. He passed the test. Now Shawndra, it is your turn."

Shawndra stepped forward and looked at Verdigris and said, "I don't understand, but I'll try to do what you ask."

Verdigris asked, "What is your greatest desire?"

Shawndra lifted her head and said, "That's easy, to be a soldier of the Citadel. Do I get to go in now?"

"No," said Verdigris, "I am not finished. What is your greatest fear?"

Shawndra was surprised at the question. She had always acted like nothing scared her, but now she had to tell the truth or she couldn't continue on the journey with her friends. She was forced to face what she had always tried to cover up. She replied, "I guess, I guess I'm afraid of everything."

Sebastian and Bolo were surprised by the answer. They had never heard Shawndra say anything that admitted weakness.

Shawndra continued, "No one believes that I can do anything other that what's expected of a girl. If I don't become a soldier one day then my dreams will be crushed, so I'm afraid of failure. But if I do become a soldier, then I will have to prove myself everyday, and if I fail once then they will say it's because I'm a girl and I shouldn't be in the Citadel. So I'm afraid of success. So I guess I'm afraid of everything."

Verdigris breathed deeply and said, "The air of truth is about you. You may enter my home." Sebastian let out a sigh of relief as Shawndra walked around Verdigris to stand behind the great Baruk. Even though she had passed the test, in some way she felt defeated.

Sebastian whispered to her, "That was great."

Shawndra whispered back, "Thanks, if you tell anyone what I said, I'll punch you in the nose."

Bolo stepped forward and said, "Well, might as well get this over with. If I don't pass and have to walk all the way back down the mountain, I might as well get started as soon as I can."

Verdigris looked deeply into Bolo and asked, "Are you brave?"

Bolo scratched his chin and said, "I don't really

see myself as brave. I mean I'm a soldier and all, but I don't particularly like to fight and I'm not as good at sneaking up on people as Ba'ar. But I guess I do what I have to. Now if you're talking about if I'm brave right now, I mean at this moment, I don't think so. I'm a little scared, with your claws and fangs and all. But I won't run away, and I can't leave my friends. Here's another thing—"

"That's enough," said Verdigris. "Being truthful is not a problem for you. You reak of honesty. You may actually be too truthful. Take your place with your friends who will enter into my home." Bolo walked around Verdigris to stand with Sebastian and Shawndra who smiled at him, happy that they would all go in together.

Captain Hart stepped forward and stood tall with his armor. Even after days of walking and fighting with little rest, he still looked like a regal soldier. "It is time for my testing."

Verdigris looked at Captain Hart as he had everyone before and asked, "Why do you regret?"

Sebastian thought this to be an odd question. Why would the captain of the Citadel regret anything? Sebastian never thought of Hart as having any weakness or flaw. Maybe this was a flaw in itself.

Captain Hart shifted his weight and looked to the ground, then to the sky, and finally into the deep dark eyes of the Baruk and said, "I once wronged a good man. I did not fulfill my duty to him, and he paid the price for my disloyalty. It is my greatest regret." These words sliced the air like a double-edged sword. The Captain admitted that he had once betrayed a man.

"That can't be, sir. This creature is trying to trick you," said Ba'ar as he stepped forward with his hand on his sword.

"Be still soldier!" commanded Captain Hart in a deep booming voice. He then returned his gaze to the Baruk and spoke in a low humble tone, "My words are true. I once betrayed a man, a man that was once a friend. I can never forgive myself."

"You speak the truth, Captain, welcome to my home," said Verdigris.

Ba'ar stepped forward and said, "I'm tired of this game. This is no test."

"If you wish to enter my home, then you will answer me truthfully, if you do not, then you will be denied," said Verdigris.

"Ask your question and see the honor of a soldier," said Ba'ar defiantly.

Verdigris looked at him and asked, "What do you love?"

Ba'ar laughed and said, "What sort of question is that? A soldier loves his duty and his country. A soldier lives to uphold the law and fight injustice. And I am a soldier."

"I know you are a soldier. I know you are supposed to love those things, but answer me truthfully. What do you love?" Verdigris could see that

Ba'ar was trying to avoid answering the question directly, but Verdigris would not allow it.

"I already told you. I love duty. I love Crespin. I love the Citadel," said Ba'ar in a serious tone as he stood up straight. He looked over to Captain Hart for some sort of reassurance that he had answered correctly, but his captain seemed more interested in Verdigris' response than Ba'ar's.

The Baruk filled his nostrils with air and opened his eyes and said, "You have spoken...a lie." Verdigris' words were heavy as all but Captain Hart gasped at such a statement. "You do not love duty, Crespin, or the Citadel. I can sense that you love power, position, and yourself. You love titles and the praise of people. Had you answered truthfully, you would have entered with us and stayed with my family tonight. However, your heart is not truthful, and I cannot trust you to keep the location of my people a secret. You must stay behind with the horse.

"What do you mean? What sort of insult is this?" cried Ba'ar. "I am a soldier of the Citadel, and I demand that you apologize for your disrespect."

Verdigris' hair on the back of his neck bristled and he showed his claws and razor sharp teeth, "You will demand nothing of me. My own tribe is full of those who have shown bravery and cowardice, who are diligent and lazy. But they are not liars. I have had but one requirement of you, and that is to be truthful. You have failed, and you will not continue." Ba'ar looked as though he were going to burst. The veins in his neck were bulging, and he had not taken his hand off of the hilt of his sword. Verdigris continued. "I warn you, little man, if you try to follow us into the mountain, we will scatter your limbs to the four corners of Crespin."

"And we will help," said a deep booming voice from above. Everyone looked up and saw that two more Baruk had crawled down the steep slope of the mountain and were just a few feet above them. Ba'ar took his hand from his sword and stepped slowly backward. The two Baruk jumped down into the space between Ba'ar and Verdigris. The one with the deep voice asked, "Who is this man that he dares to threaten one of our own? Shall I cut him in half, Verdigris?"

Verdigris turned, faced Sebastian, smiled, and winked, "I don't know, Urune. What does your mate say?"

Sebastian thought that Urune seemed a fitting name for such a creature. And he figured that it made sense that they took mates and had cubs and all of that. Sebastian had just never considered it.

"What do you think, Oolagah? Should I use his arms to clean my teeth at night?" asked Urune of the other new Baruk.

"Stop it, you two. It doesn't take a Baruk to know that this one is scared. Let's pick up those that are coming home with us and be on our way." Oolagah had a determined voice, but was lighter and seemed more caring.

Ba'ar stepped forward and shouted, "How dare

you call me scared. I am Ba'ar, second in—" Ba'ar didn't have time to react as Urune sprang forward, knocked Ba'ar off of his feet and immediately pinned him to the ground with one of his great paws.

"If you ever raise your voice to my mate, or any of our females again, I will not be merciful. I will spill your entrails where you stand." Urune's voice showed that the great Baruk was very near losing control.

"Enough, Urune," said Verdigris calmly. "We must bring these to Kronos. And that one that you have on the ground will take the horse around the base of the mountain and meet all of us at the northern base where the trail turns to Sodorrah, won't you?"

Verdigris gave a sharp look to Ba'ar, and he nodded feverishly and said, "Yes, yes sir, I'll do whatever you want."

Oolagah stepped forward and asked, "Who is my rider?"

"You shall take the captain. He has much influence with men and must be treated well," said Verdigris. "Urune, you shall take the fat one they call Bolo. Be careful with him, he has a true heart. I shall take my little brother here and the girl."

Urune asked, "What about this one?" Urune had not yet let Ba'ar off the ground. "I should really like to throw him from one of the highest peaks and then—"

"That's enough!" said Oolagah. "Stop torturing the creature and let him be."

Sebastian figured that Oolagah was the only animal that could ever speak to Urune that way. Urune backed away from Ba'ar and then knelt on the ground, as did Verdigris and Oolagah.

"Everybody, get on our backs the way I told you," said Verdigris.

"How do we? I mean do we hold onto? Where do we?" Bolo was stuttering because he didn't quite know what to do when it came to riding a Baruk.

Verdigris laughed and said, "Well, you don't ride us like a horse. When you get on our backs, lay down and put your hands around our necks and then get a hand full of our mane. Use your legs to hold on as well. None of you are wearing spurs, that's a good thing. You don't kick us or nudge us or guide us like a horse. We will take you where you need to go on the path of our choosing. All you have to do is not fall off."

"And that's easier said than done," said Urune with a devilish grin.

"I said stop torturing people, Urune," said Oolagah.

Everyone climbed onto their Baruk, and while Sebastian held onto Verdigris' neck, Shawndra held on to Sebastian's waist. The Baruk rose to their feet as if nothing were on their backs at all.

Verdigris walked to the base of the mountain and faced the sheer granite wall that Urune and Oolagah had just come down, "I'll go first. Then Oolagah and then Urune. We will meet at the entrance to the home of our Klan." Then Verdigris crouched low and said in a whisper, "Hold on little brother, hold on very tight." Sebastian then tightened his grip until his knuckles began turning white. Verdigris launched up the wall like a coiled spring that had just been loosed. His claws were digging into the rock as they raced up the mountain side.

Oolagah was next and said to Captain Hart, "You may be a great man, but if you fall off my back, your reputation won't save you from the rocks. Hold on tight." Then she and her rider began their climb in the same manor as Verdigris.

Lastly Urune approached the wall, and Bolo said, "Any last words of advice before we go?" Bolo was hoping to make friends with this Baruk and find some sort of comfort.

"Yeah!" said Urune as he crouched low to prepare for the first jump. "Don't die." Bolo grabbed on tight to Urune's neck as the Baruk jumped higher in the air than any of the others. As they traveled up the mountain jumping from boulder to boulder, the only things that could be heard was the sound of Bolo screaming and Urune laughing.

UP THE MOUNTAIN

All of the group, with the exception of Ba'ar and Balam, traveled up the granite mountains on the backs of three very powerful Baruk. Sebastian and Shawndra were on Verdigris, who was in the lead. Captain Hart was next on Oolagah, and lastly Bolo was being carried by Urune. Verdigris leaped effortlessly over great chasms in the rock. Even though they were traveling at a great speed over rough terrain, it seemed as though they glided from boulder to boulder. The rocks were etched with the claw marks of other Baruk who had made this same journey. At this point, there was no need in leaving a trail. No man could follow it. And even if he tried to follow them, it would take weeks of climbing. The Baruk were well hidden and well defended. The steep cliffs and jagged edges of the mountain itself stood as a watchman against any intruder into the secret lives of the Baruk. Sebastian thoroughly enjoyed the view from Verdigris' back while Shawndra's shrieks and moans said that she was less than thrilled. The view from the mountain cliffs was unlike any Sebastian had ever seen. From this height, he could see the winding Jezreel River snake its way through the mountains. He saw where it dropped into the valley that contained Falls Lake and the plains that extended from the mountain's edge. In the other direction, the river disappeared into rocky cliff faces, but a faint light could be seen from far off. "That is Sodorrah," said Verdigris as if he was sensing what Sebastian was thinking.

"Sodorrah, that's where we're headed," said Sebastian into Verdigris's ear. Sebastian was still clutching Verdigris's fur tightly around the neck. Verdigris leaped to the next peak and stopped their climb. "We will wait here for the others to catch up."

"Will you go with us to the city?" asked Sebastian.

"That is for the leader of our clan to decide. We will do exactly what he asks us to do," said Verdigris.

"Who is the leader of your tribe?"

"Kronos, my father."

"The one who knows my father. I would like to ask him some questions about that. There is so much I don't know about him," said Sebastian.

"All I can tell you is that he will answer what he wishes, and nothing more," said Verdigris. "You must not press him. He is not like one of your tame animals. He is a great leader, and he is accustomed to respect."

Sebastian could hear the sound of the other Baruk as their powerful claws gripped the steep slopes of the mountain, leaping from one peak to another. The Baruk carrying Captain Hart was in the lead. Urune, who carried Bolo was last. "Alas, I can smell the fear of young Bolo. He is not enjoying the view as well as you did," said Verdigris.

"And I can hear Bolo," said Sebastian as they heard Bolo's high pitched yelps as the Baruk he was riding took ever greater leaps across the wide gaps in the rocks.

Everyone arrived safely, and Verdigris looked to the group and spoke. "We are now going to descend into the home of the Baruk. You are our guests for the night, but heed my warnings if you want your stay to be a pleasant one. Do not wander far from the camp-fires. Baruk are not the only creatures in these mountains. Also, when you meet our leader, you must not approach him unless he calls. Otherwise his mates will tear you to pieces. Is that understood?"

"Quite!" said Bolo with astonishment.

"Then how will I be able to ask him about my father?" asked Sebastian.

"When we arrive, I will take you to Kronos and present you as the son of Cakal Corvin. You must step forward and kneel at the mouth of the cave in which he dwells. If he calls you to enter, you may approach and ask whatever you wish. However, if he does not request your presence, do not approach him. If you step one foot into the cave, you will not live long enough to feel regret."

"I hope he will speak with me," said Sebastian.

"I have a feeling that he will, little brother," said Verdigris.

"What about the Elder?" asked Shawndra, who had just recovered enough to speak. "When will we know how she is doing?"

Verdigris said, "Yes, the Elder. She will be fine I imagine. But the cost of her recovery will be great indeed." Verdigris lowered his head, as did the two other Baruk. "Your journey and your mission are vitally important, now more than ever, little brother. You cannot fail. You must not fail."

Captain Hart leaned forward and asked, "Why do you say this?"

Verdigris raised his head and said, "I have said too much. It is not my place to explain these things. My father will tell you all you need to know when we reach the bottom of this ravine.

"That's all assuming that we even make it to the bottom," said the Baruk that Bolo was riding as he winked to the others. "This one on my back is heavier than a thunder steed. I almost lost my footing coming up here." The Baruk turned to Oolagah with a smile.

Bolo said nervously, "Well, let's not rush getting to the bottom. I'm in no hurr—" At that moment the Baruk leaped off of the cliff and the sound of his sharp claws digging into the granite could be heard. The only thing louder than that of the claws was the screams of Bolo echoing off the mountain walls.

"If he doesn't think it's safe, then why did he jump off the cliff?" asked Shawndra.

"Young Bolo is in no danger. Urune is the strongest of us and is just having some fun with your friend," said Verdigris.

"Well, let's see this tribe of yours," said Captain Hart. The Baruk he was riding leaped off the cliff as the one before. Verdigris stepped to the edge and prepared to follow with Sebastian and Shawndra on his back.

"Are you ready, little brother?" asked Verdigris.

"I don't know. There are so many things I don't know about my father, and I am little afraid to find out," said Sebastian.

"I meant about the journey down. But I guess you are right. The journey inside one's own self is a much more treacherous route. We will be with my tribe in moments, but you will have this new knowledge about your father with you forever," said Verdigris.

"I think I'm ready, Verdigris. Let's go meet your father," said Sebastian.

"You mean our father," said Verdigris. Shawndra tightened her grip on Sebastian as Verdigris leaped off the cliff. Sebastian gave a cry of excitement while Shawndra winced from the fall. Sebastian could hear the sound of grinding rock under Verdigris' claws as they slid down the steep wall into a canyon. They were sliding right into a cave, and Sebastian called out to Verdigris, "Will we be able to see if we go in there?"

Verdigris laughed and said, "You will not, little brother, but I will see better than if we stayed in the light." In a moment, all was black and the only thing Sebastian could hear was the grinding of rock and the pounding of his heart.

———•———

Ba'ar remained standing in the same spot that the Baruk had left him when they gave him the stern warning not to follow under pain of death. How was it that an accomplished soldier, like himself, would be asked to stay behind and take care of a horse while two children and a sloppy oaf would be allowed to proceed? Ba'ar looked at Balam and thought, *He's not even a good horse. Just a puny pack horse that's only good for carrying supplies and eating grass.* The humiliation seemed more than he could bear.

Ba'ar began saying out loud, "How dare a smelly, oversized dog tell me what is true and what is false? A soldier does love his country and his duty. But a soldier also looks out for himself. Isn't that part of one's duty? What becomes of a person who goes through life only looking out for others? I'll tell you, they wind up powerless and alone. Yes, I do look out for my own well being, but that serves my land as well." Ba'ar realized that Balam was his only audience, and the horse was disinterested. Ba'ar was feeling as if he had been discarded like an unnecessary tool that is unfit for the task at hand.

Ba'ar took Balam's reins and attempted to pull him northward along the trail in the direction that Verdigris had told him. Balam did not move. The horse was no more excited about being left with Ba'ar than Ba'ar was about being left out of the adventure. "Come on, you filthy animal!" said Ba'ar. "The only reason I don't leave you here to be prey for predators is that I'd have to carry all that is in your packs myself." Ba'ar also didn't enjoy the thought of seeing Captain Hart again without the only thing he was supposed to protect. "I said move, horse!"

Ba'ar pulled Balam's reins so hard that one of them snapped, and Ba'ar fell on the ground and rolled to the edge of the trail. The drop would be steep and end in a painful landing on jagged rocks that would definitely injure and possibly kill. Ba'ar grabbed a root from a nearby plant. However it was not enough to stop him from rolling off the edge. Ba'ar was losing his grip when Balam grabbed his collar in his mouth and began pulling him back onto the trail. Once Ba'ar was safe again, he scrambled to his feet and was enraged. Not because he had lost his footing and nearly died, but that the horse had now saved his life. In disgust, Ba'ar took off his glove and struck Balam across the nose. "If you had obeyed me to begin with then I would not have fallen and you would not have had to soil my collar with your mouth." Ba'ar grabbed Balam's harness more firmly and said, "If you don't follow me this time, then I will take a lash to you." Balam relented and reluctantly followed Ba'ar's lead. They began the three-day journey around the base of the mountain where they would join the others who were traveling through the heart of the mountains and into the home of the Baruk.

———•——

Verdigris, Sebastian, and Shawndra were sliding down the steepest slope Sebastian had ever seen. They had slid into the darkness of a cave and all Sebastian could see were the sparks that came from Verdigris' mighty claws as they dug into the granite. The smell of hot embers was in the air, and as Sebastian strained his eyes as he peered into the darkness he began to see light below them. All the others in his group had already gone ahead and should be waiting for them at the bottom. Sebastian was switching between feeling overwhelmed with excitement of this great adventure and being scared for what lay next.

With a leap from the slope just before it ran out onto level ground, Verdigris landed lightly and bounded forward with Sebastian and Shawndra safely on his back. There in the waning sunlight were Captain Hart and Bolo. Bolo was hunched over as if he were sick. They had both dismounted the Baruk that had carried them. Verdigris approached them and then kneeled and said, "You must walk from here, little brother."

Sebastian and Shawndra dismounted Verdigris and joined their companions. "What's wrong with Bolo?"

"It seems that Baruk riding doesn't sit well with him," said Hart.

"That's an understatement," said Bolo. "I'm not meaning any disrespect, it was a fine ride, Urune."

Urune laughed out loud in the peculiar Baruk way. "It's not something that you need to get comfortable with. I've never allowed a man to touch me, not to mention ride on my back to my very home. Most men are not worthy of that honor. But Kronos says you must come here tonight, and so we brought you."

"Why didn't Kronos come and see us himself?" asked Captain Hart.

"Because my father is ancient and his remaining years are few. If anyone seeks his wisdom, he must travel to Kronos, and not the other way around. We must not keep him waiting," said Verdigris.

The group began walking down a rocky path through a deep valley cut into the rock by water and time. The path became so narrow with steep walls on each side that the group had no choice than to walk single file. The Baruk looked so big that they wouldn't be able to fit, but Sebastian was amazed at how they could squeeze their large bulk into such a small space. All at once the path opened up into a large valley and Sebastian saw what the Baruk were so protective of.

"It's like a garden in the middle of the mountains," said Sebastian. Sebastian was followed by Shawndra as she gasped at the bright colors of green and jade that contrasted against the dull gray of granite. There was evidence of there once being a waterfall that fell into a pool. The water seemed to have recently dried up. There were small Baruk cubs sniffing at the edges of the pool and using their front paws to scratch away at the dirt in order to find a few drops.

Eventually everyone emerged from the narrow entrance, and even Captain Hart was surprised that such life was present in the middle of a wilderness of stone. "How did you ever find this place?" asked the Captain.

"This has been the ancestral home of the Baruk since before my father. It is our greatest secret, and you are among the very few who have ever been allowed to enter in my lifetime," answered Verdigris.

The Baruk cubs, as well as most other Baruk in the valley, were now staring at their new visitors. Some had bristled at the presence of strangers, but these were mostly the young. The mature and very old looked upon them with a sort of mild neglect. These people were nothing they had not seen before in another place.

"Come on, Kronos isn't coming to you," said Urune. "Besides, there's a whole feast that's been prepared for you in your honor."

"A feast?" said Bolo. "What sort of food will be at this feast?"

"You know, snake scales with grub pudding," said Urune. "If we're lucky there will be worm root seasoned with boiled leaches, the usual sort of thing for guests. And if you don't eat every bit, it's an insult and you will be ripped—"

Urune was interrupted by an approaching Baruk. "Urune, stop that at once. Why do you keep bothering the young human with such stories?"

Urune replied, "What stories, you couldn't even hear what I was saying from over there."

"I could tell by the color of that boy's face that you were up to no good," said the new Baruk to their party. Indeed Bolo was turning green at the prospect of eating worms, snake scales and leaches.

Urune laughed aloud again and said, "You are right, I shouldn't bother them so. Allow me to introduce to you my mother, and the provider of your meal tonight, Kidron."

Kidron bowed low and said, "Welcome, guests of Kronos. It is my honor to serve you."

"Does that mean that we won't be eating...that stuff that Urune talked about?" said Bolo.

"Of course not," said Kidron. "You will have wild lamb, boiled with mountain potatoes and seasoned with dill and sage. I am almost done, and then we will feast together," said Kidron.

"That's a relief!" said Bolo. Sebastian and Shawndra both laughed while Captain Hart looked on smiling. Hart turned and was surveying the valley and noting its superb defenses. Every corner had a guard on it. The play of the cubs and the sleeping Baruk on the lush grass made it easy to overlook the fact that every inch of the valley was watched. The

Baruk were ever vigilant and Captain Hart figured that every one of these creatures knew how to fight. Any attacking force would be seen from a distance. If they didn't try to come over the mountains then they would have to enter the valley through the narrow entrance that the rest of the group entered. Any enemy would be cut down one at a time as they emerged from the narrow slit.

"Kidron," said Verdigris, "you may recognize this one." Verdigris looked to Sebastian. Sebastian stood motionless as he had done when he first met Verdigris.

Kidron walked over to him and said, "Now why would I recognize this man cub? He's too young to have visited here before. But still, there is something familiar." Kidron drew in a deep breath and took in Sebastian's scent, and her eyes opened wide, as did Verdigris' when he realized whose son Sebastian was. "It can't be. Well bless me, you are the son of Cakal, aren't you?"

"Yes ma'am," said Sebastian respectfully.

"Little man, I am not a ma'am. I am a Baruk. Let your yes be yes and your no be no. If you are the son of Cakal, then you and Verdigris are..."

"Brothers!" said Verdigris.

"Well, does Kronos know?" asked Kidron.

"He did not tell me that the son of Cakal was in the group. We will know later," said Verdigris.

"Tonight will be interesting," said Kidron. "I have to get back to the meal. Take them to the assembly area; a large fire has been lit and your places are set," said Kidron as she turned and quickly trotted down the valley.

"Tonight you will speak with Kronos," said Verdigris. "You will need food and supplies to continue your journey to Sodorrah. And if he sees fit, you will have an escort to the edge of the city."

Shawndra quickly jumped in and asked, "What of Lady Jeanine? When will we see her again?"

Verdigris looked at her and smiled, "The Elder is under our care. Many things have happened here that you will need to know. Have trust in us that we will tell you everything you need to know in the fullness of time. But for now, let us make our way to the great assembly and take our place at the dinner fire."

Ba'ar and Balam had been walking north for several hours on the trail at the base of the mountain. The steep edges had leveled out and a sprawling forest was on his left and a granite wall on his right. He saw a faint glow near the trail in a clearing, and as he approached he could see that it was a campfire. He led Balam off the trail and tied his reins to the limb of a tree. "I don't want you getting us into trouble while I go see who this fire belongs to," said Ba'ar.

With his hand on the hilt of his sword, Ba'ar stealthily approached the fire and then saw a shadowy figure sitting on the base of a fallen tree warming itself by the flames. Ba'ar emerged out of the darkness quickly and approached the stranger and said in a commanding tone, "Who are you? Identify yourself!"

The stranger seemed startled and almost fell over backward on the log. "I am no one of great interest. I am certainly not a threat. I'm merely a traveler from Sodorrah looking for a safe path south." The stranger had his dark cloak wrapped around him, and his hood was pulled low over his face. Ba'ar could not make out his frame or his features but guessed by his startled nature that he wasn't dangerous.

"I am a soldier from Falls Lake. I am an officer of the Citadel and will stay with you and protect you tonight." Ba'ar didn't have nearly as much interest in protecting this uninteresting traveler as he did in not having to build his own fire or sleep in the cold. Ba'ar retrieved Balam and led him to the edge of the clearing. There the horse stopped and would not take another step.

Ba'ar dropped the reins and said to the horse, "I'm done leading you for the night. If you won't do as I say, then I won't bother taking off your packs. You can eat the grass here, and I'll enjoy the fire alone." Ba'ar walked to the stranger's fire and dropped his rucksack to the ground, unbuckled his belt that held his sword and dagger and began unhinging his armor. He looked to the shadowy stranger and asked, "Who are you, and what are you doing here?"

The hooded figure responded, "I am a traveler on this trail, resting, and writing poetry, and waiting for you."

Ba'ar half turned to the stranger and asked in a

confused tone, "How could you be waiting for me, you don't even know me."

"I don't have to know you in order to wait for you. I wait for all people, walking down many trails. Would you like to hear my poetry?" asked the traveler.

"I'm not much in the mood for poetry," said Ba'ar.

The mysterious person tilted his head back and wailed into the air a gruesome sound that was like a mixture of pain and torture. Ba'ar stepped back away from the fire and picked up his sword. There were echoes of the sound all around, and it seemed as if others were calling back to him from the darkness in a sad symphony of despair.

"Did you like it?" asked the hooded man.

"Like what?" asked Ba'ar who was growing more confused by the moment.

"Did you like my poem?" asked the traveler. "Of course that wasn't the whole poem and I wasn't expecting the others to join in, but I think it's quite...good."

"That was your poem? That was just a bit of shrieking and echoes. It sounded like someone speared a boar," said Ba'ar.

"Did you really think it sounded like a pierced boar? That's quite a compliment," said the traveler with an eerie smile that could be seen spreading across the lower half of his face. Ba'ar could not see all of his face, but he could make out the grayish color to his skin and the blackness around his lips.

The traveler's eyes were hidden by his hood. The traveler's cloak was dark but not quite black. Ba'ar could see that it was once a well made traveler's cloak that could have been a deep red color. However, through years of wear and neglect, the original color had faded, and the dirt and filth had changed it into a dirty robe that only hinted at its former beauty.

"How is that a compliment?" asked Ba'ar as he moved closer to the fire. Balam remained at the wood's edge. The young horse didn't want to be anywhere near this mysterious hooded figure, but he had no where to go since Ba'ar was obviously intent on remaining.

"To be able to write a poem that resembles the death struggle of a dieing animal is great indeed," said the traveler.

"You are a strange one," said Ba'ar as he took his hand off of his sword and walked more easily to the fire to warm himself. "These woods are full of bandits and thieves, and I will stay here with you for the night and share your fire," said Ba'ar as he pulled a fallen log closer to the fire and sat down.

"I don't fear what's in the darkness," said the traveler. "I've traveled these roads many times and have never had an incident with those that live in the shadows."

"How can that be?" asked Ba'ar. "My companions and myself have been attacked twice just down the road and have barely made it out with our lives."

The dark man smiled and said, "You must be

very brave." Ba'ar straightened and looked intently into the fire. "Where are the companions of which you speak? Have they become lost, or even killed?" said the traveler with a morbid anticipation. Balam began pawing the ground at the wood's edge. It was as if the horse was trying to warn Ba'ar to stop sharing so much with this mysterious stranger.

"We have chosen to part ways, temporarily of course. They have traveled into the mountain while I will take the supplies around the base, and we will meet in a place closer to Sodorrah," said Ba'ar.

The dark stranger leaned closer to the fire and Ba'ar could make out his dark eyes. Even the whites of his eyes seemed polluted and gray. "I can't believe that they would part with a warrior of your skill and bravery only to guard a horse and some food. That horse must be of some great value."

Ba'ar laughed out loud and said, "That horse is a nuisance and nothing more. He is a foolish animal that is not worth his hide."

"Are you willing to sell him?" said the traveler, as he pulled his hand from a pocket in his cloak to reveal several gold nuggets. They were oddly shaped as if they had been melted from another form and poured out to cool. "I will pay handsomely for a young horse."

"Where did you come across so much gold?" questioned Ba'ar in astonishment. Some of the old folk in the small towns surrounding Falls Lake spoke of a time when there were riches in the land of Crespin. But all of Ba'ar's life he only knew of poverty among the masses. Some people had more goats or cattle than others, but no one had silver or gold to spare.

"Gold is easy to find, that is, if your mind is free to find it," said the traveler.

"Who are you; what is your name?" said Ba'ar.

"Where are my manors? We've been sharing a fire, and I've even shared my poetry with you, and I haven't told you my name. I am Nabal. What is your name?"

"I am Ba'ar, second in command of the Citadel that guards Falls Lake." Ba'ar never just gave his name. He always gave his rank or accomplishment when meeting someone. He didn't want a stranger to mistake him for a common guard.

"Well Ba'ar, what do you say to me buying your horse? I need an animal to walk with me, and occasionally I get the taste for some fresh meat and that animal of yours looks delicious."

Balam was uneasy at the edge of the firelight near the trees. The animal didn't know what was being said but something about Nabal made him uneasy and skittish.

"I'm afraid I need the horse for now. We have many more days of travel and I don't want to carry his packs myself," said Ba'ar with a laugh. "If it wasn't for that, I would surely sell you the horse. It is worthless to me."

The shadowy stranger leaned forward and produced a black carrying bag from behind the log he was sitting on. He reached into it with his pale hand

and took out a shiny bronze goblet. The outside of goblet had been polished to a high shine and every detail had been cared for. Ba'ar couldn't help but admire the cup and thought that it seemed out of place in the hands of such an odd stranger. As Ba'ar leaned closer to get a better look, he noticed that the inside of the cup was pitch black and looked as though it had never been cleaned. He then realized that a pungent rotten smell was coming from the inside of the cup that made his nose wrinkle and he pulled away quickly.

Nabal's small mouth spread out in a grin at Ba'ar's response. "Don't you like my favorite cup? Is it not beautiful to behold?"

Ba'ar raised his arm to cover his nose and protect it from the foul odor. "Yes, beautiful on the outside, but rotten on the inside. You don't actually drink from that, do you?"

Nabal jerked his head to the side and looked directly at Ba'ar with hurt in his eyes. "Of course I drink from it. What does it matter that the inside of the cup is tarnished? All anyone ever cares about is the outside anyway." Nabal scooted closer to Ba'ar, startling him at being so close to such an odd fellow. Nabal leaned close and said in a lower, more piercing tone, "I see that your armor is very shiny and well maintained. Tell me, do you ever take care of the inside?"

Ba'ar squared his shoulders and responded with a tone of certainty, "Of course I oil the inner leather and polish the buckles you do not see. That is part of what is expected of a soldier."

Nabal responded even quicker, "I was not talking about cleaning the inside of the armor. You, young sir. You are what is inside the armor. What do you do to clean your heart? What do you do to clean your mind? What do you do to clean your conscience?"

Nabal's words struck Ba'ar harder than a hammer thrust. He felt unsure of how to answer such a question. Polishing swords and oiling leather were easy in comparison to keeping one's conscience clear. Every thought must be taken captive. Every desire and motivation must be wrestled. It was a warfare of a different kind. Ba'ar was skilled at hand to hand combat, but he was completely unarmed when it came to the war of the soul.

Nabal saw the uncertainty of the young soldier and said, "Do not lose courage, young master. My words mean nothing when compared to your great strength."

Ba'ar felt that there was hidden purpose in Nabal's words. Ba'ar's strong shoulders had slumped, his eyes down cast and he now felt very, very tired. "I think I will get my blanket and sleep here by the fire. I didn't realize until just now how tired I really am." Ba'ar walked over to Balam and pulled his blanket out and began to unload the horse's saddlebags. As he unhooked the buckles that secured the packs on the horse's back he patted Balam on the neck. Ba'ar said in a lowered tone to the animal, "We've both had a long day, and I guess you deserve some rest from your load."

Just then the shadowy figure came up beside

Ba'ar without a sound and said, "Careful young master, compassion for the weak can be a weakness in itself. Remember, this is a beast that you just said you had no use for."

The moment of tenderness soon left Ba'ar as he retightened the lashings for the pack and stepped back from the horse. "You're right. The mangy animal can keep the packs on all night for all I care." Ba'ar turned, walked back to the fire, spread out his blanket and laid down to sleep.

Nabal, still standing by Balam, said to himself, "That's it boy; that polished armor can't hide your dark heart. Nabal then lifted up the shiny goblet and removed a flask from under his cloak. He poured the contents into the filthy inside of the cup and the smell made Balam try to pull away, but Nabal grabbed his reins and kept him close. "That's right, my little horse, you know what this is." Balam pulled harder against the reins and whinnied loudly but Ba'ar would not lift his head to see what was wrong. Nabal looked at the horse as he lifted the cup to his lips and drank deep of its contents. Dark streaks of the liquid ran down his face and his grey skin streaked black as he lowered the cup. Had Ba'ar seen that Nabal was able to drink the dead water and not be paralyzed by its effects, he would know he had real reason to fear this stranger. He would know that this was no chance meeting in the dark.

THE HOME OF THE BARUK

The sun had long since set behind the towering peaks of the granite mountains. The light from the roaring fire in the Baruk camp played against the surrounding steep stone walls. The smell of roasted meat was in the air as several pikes with thick slabs of meat were held over the flames. When the meat on one of the long pikes was done, a Baruk would take hold of the base of the pike with its powerful jaws and pull the meat from the fire. Out of respect for their guests, Sebastian, Shawndra, Bolo, and Captain Hart would be allowed to cut away a portion of the cooked meat before it was laid on a large flat round stone for all of the rest of the Baruk to tear apart with their teeth and sharp claws.

Sebastian noticed that with every portion of meat, some was taken to a cave halfway up one of the granite walls. The Baruk carrying the meat would take it to the entrance to the cave and then lay down on its belly and then crawl inside. Moments later, it would crawl out and return to the feast to take more meat to the cave.

Sebastian leaned over to Shawndra and said, "I wonder where they are taking all of that food."

Shawndra sat up straight while carefully picking a piece of fat off the meat she had taken, "It's probably the leader they keep referring to. I think they said his name was Kronos. By the way those other Baruk have been crawling in and out of there while the cave is clearly not that small, seems to indicate to me that something or someone of great importance is in there."

Sebastian turned and looked back up at the cave and then to Shawndra, "Speaking of important, I haven't seen Lady Jeanine."

Shawndra had a very concerned look come over her face and said, "Me neither. I'm actually beginning to worry about her. Until now, I've kept on telling myself that she is so powerful that I shouldn't worry about her. But after what happened with the dead water, I can now see that she can be harmed.

Sebastian leaned past Shawndra and called out to Bolo, "Bolo, hey, Bolo."

Bolo had a mouthful of the most tender meat he had ever tasted. He turned to Sebastian and managed to mumble out, "Have you ever had anything so good in all your life?"

Sebastian replied, "Forget about the food; have you seen Lady Jeanine?"

Bolo swallowed down what was in his mouth and said, "No, and I've been keeping an eye out for her."

Shawndra said, "Oh sure, I've seen how you've been watching. One eye on the food and the other on seconds."

Captain Hart had also been eating, but he never stopped surveying their camp. He didn't even look down when he cut the meat or poured himself more water. He kept a keen eye on all things that were around. "Steady yourself, Sebastian," he said. "The Elder is not so easily dismissed. We will see her sooner or later. And my bet is that it will be sooner."

Sebastian was not comforted by the captain's words. He wanted to know where his friend was and when he could see her again.

"Hello, little brother," said a voice from behind Sebastian. It was Skiatook.

Sebastian jumped to his feet and asked in an excited voice, "How is Lady Jeanine? Is she all right? Can I see her? Where is she?"

Skiatook lowered himself to the ground and said to Sebastian, "All your questions will be answered in time. But for now, let's just say she is fine."

Sebastian put his fists firmly on his waist and said with the sternest voice he could muster, "You keep calling me brother and saying I can be trusted, but you won't give me any straight answers. I am growing weary of this."

Skiatook turned his head sideways and raised his ears in surprise. He had never heard of a human speaking with so little fear to a Baruk before. "There is steel in your blood after all, little brother. I told you that I could not give you the answers that you seek, only our great father and leader of our klan could do that. But now the time has arrived. Get on my back again and I will take you to Kronos. There he will answer all he cares to answer, and not a question more."

Sebastian ran around to Skiatook's side and grabbed on to the thick fur around his neck and swung himself onto the Baruk's back. Skiatook stood up as if Sebastian's weight made no difference in his strength.

Shawndra had stood up and asked, "How long will you be gone, Sebastian?"

Skiatook answered, "As long as our father wills it." And with those words he trotted off to the base of the granite wall where the cave Sebastian had noticed other Baruk taking food earlier. Skiatook leaped to one boulder and then another and on the third leap he landed at the entrance to the cave.

Sebastian had held on tightly and noted that no man, without the aid of several ladders could climb up to this height. But Skiatook did it effortlessly.

Skiatook lowered himself as before and said, "From here you go alone. Remember, Kronos is great and powerful and must be treated with respect. When you enter the cave, lay down on your belly and wait for him to call you."

Sebastian asked, "What if he doesn't call me?"

Skiatook replied, "Then don't enter. But he is the one that has summoned you, so you don't have much to fear."

"Much?" said Sebastian. "What do you mean by much?"

Skiatook answered, "Well, if you behave stupidly and don't do exactly what I've told you and you try to approach Kronos without his permission, his mates will tear you to pieces."

"Oh," said Sebastian. "That's what you mean by much."

Skiatook raised himself and said, "Now go on. Don't keep our great father waiting." He then jumped down in the same manor that he had come up.

Sebastian turned to the cave entrance and could see nothing inside. He took a step forward and then tripped over a small ridge at the mouth of the cave and as he stumbled to regain his balance he kicked a rock that flew into the darkness. As the rock disappeared into the lair, he waited for the sound of the rock hitting the ground but heard nothing. Sebastian then heard a deep sigh from inside the cave. He tried to see anything as he peered into the darkness and then remembered Skiatook's words. Sebastian quickly lowered himself onto his stomach. As his eyes adjusted to the darkness, he began to make out vague shapes. Directly in front of him were two great eyes staring at him. Sebastian froze in fear as the voice said, "I was wondering when you would come."

Sebastian could see more details of the cave with every passing moment. He saw the small rock that he had kicked lying beside a large, older looking Baruk. Sebastian assumed that was Kronos. Sebastian's other senses were now becoming finely tuned to the dark as he could hear breathing all around him. Sebastian's mind raced with thoughts, *What if he says nothing to me? What if the rock hit him and I have insulted him? I wonder if I will feel anything when the other Baruk rip me apart?* Sebastian remained motionless on the ground hoping not to offend the Baruk any more than he already had.

"Enter, my son," were the words that came from the cave.

Sebastian replied, "I'm sorry about the rock, sir. I hope you weren't sleeping. I didn't mean any offence."

Again the voice called to him, "Stand to your feet and enter. You are safe here."

Sebastian stood up slowly. He didn't want anyone, or anything, to misinterpret his actions as being aggressive.

"Come closer and let me see you." The low voice reflected its age. There was no fear or excitement in it. But there was power.

Sebastian walked slowly forward into the darkness. Then, suddenly from behind him a great light illuminated all of the cave. One of the Baruk had retrieved a burning torch from the fire in the middle of the camp where everyone was eating. Sebastian could see that there were nine Baruk in the cave with him. There were four on each side of the cave and one in the back which was Kronos.

"The light is for your benefit," said Kronos. "We can see in the dark, just as well as the light."

Sebastian said meekly while not sure what to do with his hands. "Thank you for that."

Kronos raised his head and breathed deeply the air in the cave. Upon doing this, he rose slowly and unsteadily onto his feet. His body was not as lean as the other Baruk Sebastian had seen. He showed the marks of age and experience. Sebastian noticed a long scar on his hip where no fur had grown. The more he looked, the more he realized there were many scars.

As Kronos stood, Sebastian could see his full size and could feel himself tremble. Kronos approached Sebastian and leaned his large head inches from Sebastian's head. Sebastian held his breath as he heard footsteps moving around him. The Baruk were anxious to hear the words of Kronos. Then Kronos spoke. "You have the scent of your father." At these words, three of the Baruk in the room laid down on the ground and became busy with grooming themselves. The other five left the room and paid Sebastian no more attention.

Sebastian looked around quite puzzled and turned to the aged Kronos. "How is it that everyone knows my father?"

Kronos returned to the place where he had been laying. It was a bed of soft animal skins, piled in such a manor that the old Baruk could recline but still see the entrance to the cave. The Baruk made the sort of noise that old people make as he laid down and situated himself. "I've long looked forward to telling you tales about your father, my son. I had hoped Cakal would be here for the telling. But that is part of the reason you are here to begin with."

Sebastian did not move from his spot. However, he sensed that the ancient creature was willing to indulge his curiosity, and Sebastian was going to take full advantage and get whatever answers he could. "How is it that you call me son and your sons call me brother?"

Kronos pushed a pile of animal skins out in front of him and said, "Come, sit here. The time for questions and answers is upon us."

Sebastian surprised himself with how quickly he ran to the spot Kronos had made for him. He was just a couple of feet from the old Baruk and the answers to so many mysteries.

Kronos peered intently into Sebastian's eyes and said, "You are indeed my son. Just as my sons are your brothers. Many years ago before your birth, and before the dead water came and poisoned the land, your father was a captain at the Citadel. He served the king and enforced all of his decrees." Kronos leaned forward and lowered his voice to emphasize what he was about to say. "You see, Sebastian, not all creatures that drink from the living water that flows from the cave of the source are changed in the same way. Some are just healthier. Others are changed much more profoundly. Others learn to speak. We learn to reason. We are not only animals, but also something more."

Sebastian's eyes were wide as he took in every word. "You are intelligent."

"Yes!" said Kronos excitedly. "The great king under the mountain chooses certain of us to think and to speak. We are able to choose and discern wisdom from folly. And this sets us apart from other creatures. The King of Crespin, whom your father served, recognized this. He made a law that any creature capable of speech was not to be hunted. We were to be left alone to seek out the will of Mai. But not all the people in the land of Crespin would follow the king's words. The dark lords of men took council together and decided to hire other men to hunt the Baruk for our skins and for our teeth. This caused the Baruk to despise men and retreat deep into the mountain to raise our young.

Sebastian said, "The dark lords. Do you mean the members of the Ivveleth? Our judges?"

Kronos continued, "Yes. Your judges paid handsomely for our fur. The king sent your father and his soldiers to the base of the mountains where we hunted to keep trappers away from us. It was there that I met Cakal Corvin. I was hungry and had stopped being careful in the hunt. I did not see the trap until it was too late. Once I was snared, I could not run away. The trap was staked to the ground, and men with spears jumped from the bushes. One ran at me with his sword, but I cut him down easily. The others learned from the fool and stayed out of my reach. They hurled their spears and pierced my side and hip. I was too wounded to fight and I knew that my skin would be someone else's prize. That is when your father arrived. As the hunters closed in on me and drew their skinning knives I heard the hooves of your father's horse as he rode into the midst of the men and commanded them to leave. They did not take kindly to his words. One man from behind him speared him in the back. Cakal fell to the ground beside me but managed to get to his feet. He drew his sword and defended me for as long as his strength held. Of the twelve hunters, three of them escaped to the woods, without their prize. The rest died by the blade of your father.

Sebastian was listening intently. He had never heard such a story. Not even the fishermen, known for their elaborate tales of great catches, had ever told anything like this.

Kronos continued. "The next thing I remember is waking up to the sound of a sweet voice singing a healing song. My strength was returning, and an old woman was standing before me. She told me that your father had defended me until he could not stand anymore. He did what he could to stop my bleeding but we were both too seriously wounded. Had the Elder not come along, we would have both died. I looked to your father, lying by my side and I saw that our blood had run together on the ground. That day I pledged that my line would be forever bound to your father and his house. And this meeting tonight is in honor of that pledge."

Sebastian laid back against the rugs and let out a deep breath. He had been holding his breath almost the entire time. He was finally beginning to understand all the mysteries surrounding his life. But there was so much more to know. "Can I ask you something else?"

Kronos laid his powerful head on his bed of animal skins and said, "You may ask anything you wish, I may not answer it. But you may ask none the less."

Sebastian sat forward again, "Where is Lady Jeanine?"

"Ah, that is a very good question. And you deserve an answer," said Kronos. "The power of the Elders flows from the Great Mai through the living water. Since the dead water has come, there is no fresh source for the Elders to renew their strength. Also, the Baruk must regularly drink from the living water in order to be able to speak and reason. We were able to keep a pool of living water here in our home for some time. When you entered our home, you noticed a dried up pool, did you not? That is were the water was kept. There was precious little left, but when my son, Skiatook, brought us the Elder, we knew that we must use our last few precious drops to restore her strength. Her life was fading fast as the dead water was taking her. We placed her in the pool, and it took all that we had in order to make her strong enough to travel again."

Sebastian said with excitement, "So she is all right?"

"Yes," said Kronos. "She will be fine. She is resting. She needs to drink from the purest water soon, but she has enough strength to lead you to the cave of the source."

Sebastian said, "I didn't know if we had lost her or not. I don't think I could…" Sebastian paused as a look of horror came over his face. "Wait a minute. If she took all of your living water, what will happen to you? What will happen to your cubs? What about your sons?" Sebastian was beginning to panic.

Kronos raised his head and leaned close to Sebastian. "Now you know why you are so important. For some reason Mai has chosen you at this time to cleanse the water. You must not fail. The truth of it is that the life in the pool we had was fading. More and more of our kind have been wandering into the mountains. There are rumors that they have been captured by men who are sickened by the dead water. The only hope for them, and for any of us is you, Sebastian. If you fail, my kind are doomed. You must find a way to cleanse the spring and bring life again to my kind."

Sebastian said, "But I don't know what's wrong with the water. I'm not even sure Lady Jeanine knows. How am I—" Sebastian was not allowed to finish his question.

"I know the blood that flows in your veins is strong. I know that you are very much like your father. Just as your father saved me many years ago, you will save my people. You may not believe in yourself, but I believe in you. Trust that Mai will direct your path." Kronos laid his head back down and breathed heavily.

Sebastian moved closer and placed his hand on Kronos' shoulder. "Are you all right?"

Kronos smiled and said, "You have given me hope. Now, let's have no more questioning for the night. We both need to rest because tomorrow your journey begins again." Sebastian laid down against the warm Baruk and fell into a deep sleep there at his side. He knew that the safest place in all of Crespin was in the home of this Baruk, the wildest and noblest of all creatures.

AROUND THE CAMPFIRE

The night had ended with a new revelation about Sebastian's father. Sebastian had thought of him as a coward who couldn't bear to stay in Falls Lake and face his wife's death, and the prospect of raising a son alone. However, Sebastian was now finding that his father was more than just a man. He was a hero to many living creatures in Crespin.

Sebastian woke to the sound of raspy breathing. Sebastian had fallen asleep on the many rugs that made up the bed of Kronos. Kronos himself was experiencing the half sleep of the Baruk. None of them ever seemed to be fully asleep. When their eyes were closed, their ears were alert and attentive to any noise that was not natural to the quiet mountains. Throughout the night, Baruk scouts traveled up and down the paths that led to the high places on the surrounding peaks and beyond. Sebastian had never felt so secure.

As he looked out across the valley, he saw something that surprised him. The same old man that he had seen with Lady Jeanine before they left Falls Lake was now sitting on a rock and being served by Skiatook. Lady Jeanine was talking with him, and Urune was listening attentively. As Sebastian watched, he saw something even more peculiar. Both Lady Jeanine and Urune bowed to the dirty man as he stood, finishing his food, and then climbed onto the back of another Baruk that Sebastian had not seen before. With a jolt, the Baruk, with his strange companion, sprinted across the valley and disappeared on the other side.

Sebastian was leaning forward and trying to make sense of it when he heard the voice of Kronos beside him say, "Have you seen that man before?"

"Yes, in Falls Lake. Just before we left, he was talking with Lady Jeanine, and she bowed to him. I've never seen that before," said Sebastian.

Kronos did not raise his head this time when he spoke. "Did he give you anything?"

Sebastian knew he shouldn't be surprised any more about how much Kronos knew about anything, but how could he know about the dagger? "Yes. He gave me this." Sebastian took the blade from inside his cloak.

"Good," said Kronos. He gave a weak smile and looked at Sebastian. "You keep up with that blade, my boy. It's a key to more than just a wall. It is unusual to see an Elder bow to anyone, especially one with such a lowly appearance," said Kronos.

"Why did Urune bow to him? I wouldn't think that a Baruk would bow to any man."

"You are correct, young Sebastian," said Kronos. "We Baruk do not bow to just any man. We would bow out of respect for your father, we would bow for respect of the Elder, and we would bow out of respect for that man," said Kronos.

"You know who he is? Then please, Kronos, please tell me who he is," pleaded Sebastian.

"I have told you many things about the past that concern you and me. But that man's story is not mine to tell. When the time is right, you will know the truth behind all the things you have seen," said Kronos, as he shifted his powerful head to a more comfortable position.

"When will the time be right?" asked Sebastian.

"The time will be right when you are ready to do something with the story you will hear. But until then, don't worry about what you don't know. Your hands are full enough with what you do know. Now, I hear my son's approach, I'm sure the time is near for you to return to your journey," said Kronos.

Skiatook, eldest son of Kronos, came into the cave and lay on his belly and said, "Great father, all preparations have been made for your sons to continue to the city of Sodorrah. We ask your blessing to leave."

Without moving Kronos said, "My blessing is

given. Continue with all haste, my sons." Kronos closed his eyes and let out a deep breath. The raspy breathing that awoke Sebastian was coming from Kronos. He was getting weaker.

Sebastian and Skiatook left the cave. As they stood at its mouth, Skiatook lowered himself as Sebastian climbed onto his back. Sebastian said, "Will the living water heal your father?"

Skiatook said, "He is your father as well. The water will extend his life, but our great father is very advanced in years and his time is coming."

"Well then," said Sebastian as he grabbed on tight to Skiatook. "We haven't a moment to lose. Let's get to Sodorrah."

———•———

Ba'ar awoke to the sounds of screeching and wailing. He jumped up from the ground only to see that the dark and oily stranger whose camp he had shared seemed to be rolling on the ground in great pain.

"What is wrong with you?" yelled Ba'ar. "Were you bitten by an asp? Did you fall and break something?"

Nabal rolled onto his knees and cried out, "I am just enjoying a marvelous breakfast." The man began to cough and wheeze, and his face twisted in pain. He then picked up a small rock, placed it in his mouth and then bit down on it. Upon doing this, his shrieks of pain began again.

"Why are you chewing on rocks?" asked Ba'ar

in amazement. "I can hear your teeth breaking to pieces. Stop doing that!"

The grey-skinned man jumped to his feet and thrust his bony pale finger into Ba'ar's face and said, "Who are you to tell me what is right and what is wrong? I say that rocks and sand make a fit breakfast. I say that pain is pleasure and pleasure is pain."

"You are a loony!" said Ba'ar. "You'll die if you keep on doing that."

"No, I have done this for many years, thirteen to be exact. And I have yet to die. I have learned the secret to limitless power. I have captured the knowledge of the Elders and used it to grow stronger. I know the secrets that give glory to those with the will to seize it." The stranger then regained his composure and slid his hood back over his grey skinned head.

Ba'ar leaned closer and asked, "What do you mean, 'the secret to limitless power'?"

"Ahh," said Nabal. "You are interested in power. But that is to be expected from one with such skill."

For the first time in a long time, Ba'ar was now interested in what someone else had to say. "You speak of power, fame, and glory. How can someone like you understand these things?"

Nabal sat down on the ground and said, "The water that flows out of the mountain comes from the cave of the source, does it not?"

"Yes, that is what the Elders say," said Ba'ar

"Well, whether living or dead, the water has great power. But only if you have the soul to contain it.

Only a person called to drink of the living water by the Great Mai may drink from the source and receive power to be an Elder. This we all know. But since the living power of the water is gone and death has now taken its place, a different kind of person is needed to drink and receive power. A soul that is absolutely dead inside. A soul that uses the power of the dead water to his benefit. What do you think, my young soldier? Does this not make sense?" Nabal leaned close and watched Ba'ar's brow wrinkle as he thought about these things.

Ba'ar said, "Are you telling me that you can drink the dead water? How can that be; you are not dead?"

"There is much you don't know, but much I can teach you, Ba'ar," Nabal said. "Think about it, the Elder Jeanine wants you to help change the dead water back to the living water. Why? I'll tell you, because she is powerless without it. She wants to rule Crespin with her weak followers at her side. You can't let that happen."

Ba'ar leaned away from Nabal and said, "What do you mean? Elders don't want to govern. All they ever do is give their useless advice."

Nabal grabbed Ba'ar's arm, and it startled him. Nabal pulled him close, "No, that's not how they rule. She will place that sniveling child, Sebastian, in charge and rule through him. He will be her puppet, that is if they cleanse the source. But I can think of a better ruler for Crespin. Someone with the strength to rule all creatures. Someone skilled in fighting. You, Ba'ar, you should rule, not a child and an old woman."

Ba'ar began to pull away, but he surprised himself that he didn't pull away too hard. "Are you saying I can drink the dead water and become as powerful as an Elder?"

Nabal smiled wickedly and said, "No, at least not now. But I will teach you. But only if you rejoin your group and go with them to the cave of the source. Go and keep them from purifying the stream."

Ba'ar could imagine himself a great and powerful leader, with all of Crespin at his command. He could rule all the other cadets at the Citadel absolutely. He saw himself with a crown and a long cavalry sword on top of the strongest of horses. But then he realized that in order to do this, he would have to betray the orders of Captain Hart. He would have to oppose his commander and risk being shamed. As skilled as Ba'ar was, he was no match for the experienced Captain. Ba'ar pulled away harshly and broke free of Nabal's grip. "This is foolishness. It is time for me to get underway and rejoin my group." Ba'ar scooped up the blanket he slept on during the night and then hastily fastened his light armor about him.

Nabal sat quietly until Ba'ar took Balam's reins and began leading him toward the trail that would take him around the base of the mountain. Then Nabal called out, "Your father would see the wisdom of my words. We will speak again, Ba'ar."

Ba'ar turned back to reply but Nabal had disappeared into the woods. Ba'ar pulled Balam's reins and tried to brush off the unpleasantness of the morning. If he kept walking and took very little rest, he could be at the river crossing to Sodorrah by nightfall.

———•———

Skiatook carried Sebastian to the far end of the valley that housed the Baruk. Hart, Shawndra, and Bolo were there waiting for him, already mounted on the backs of Baruk. When Skiatook joined them with Sebastian as his rider, he asked, "Where is the Elder?"

"Verdigris is bringing the wise one. She has final words to share with Kronos before we leave," said Urune.

Sebastian asked, "Has anyone spoken to her since we've been here?"

"None of us," said Shawndra.

Skiatook replied, "She will tell you everything when you are ready to hear it. Until then, I don't think you should press her."

Captain Hart spoke up, "I agree. Our next and most important goal is to reach the river east of Sodorrah by nightfall. Then we can camp in the city and then go upstream to the cave of the source."

Bolo said, "That's a long way to travel in one day. Maybe we can take it a little slower and arrive there tomorrow. What do you say to that, Urune? Going slower?"

Urune grunted and said, "Just for that I think I will

try to make Sodorrah in a half light's travel." Bolo sighed with disappointment and looked as though he was turning green just imagining the leaps over large ledges and the near death experiences.

Captain Hart spied another Baruk coming their way and saw Lady Jeanine riding on his back. "Steady yourself, Bolo. Our journey is about to begin again."

Verdigris, who carried the Elder, arrived with the group. Lady Jeanine had the appearance of a young strong woman again but she looked weary. She did not have the glow she had at the beginning of the journey from Falls Lake. "There is no time to lose," said the Elder. "A report has come to me that the city of Sodorrah is in peril. Mountain people who have been poisoned by the dead water have attacked and overrun the city. They are dragging the townsfolk out and forcing them to drink the dead water. There are precious few left who have not been taken. We must leave immediately."

Sebastian desperately wanted to speak with Jeanine privately. He wanted to know how his beloved Elder was feeling. He wanted to know if she was going to be all right. He was trying to catch a glimpse from her, but she avoided his gaze. All the Baruk and their riders turned to the base of the mountain. and one by one they all leaped into air, clawing their way from ledge to ledge, leaving the safety of their home.

Finally, Sebastian finally couldn't keep quiet anymore. Just before Skiatook began to climb Sebastian said, "Wait!" He turned to Lady Jeanine and asked, "I need to know. Are you going to be okay?

Lady Jeanine's stern face softened and she smiled. "Yes, Sebastian. All will be well. We can't talk now, but we will. The people of Sodorrah need us."

Sebastian nodded, and Skiatook and Verdigris leaped up the mountain.

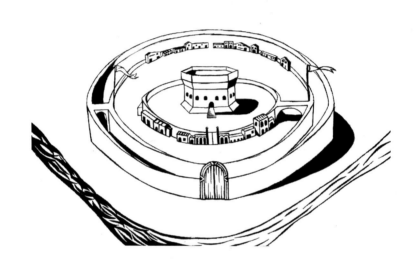

RETAKING SODORRAH

The evening light was waning in the sky and Ba'ar was approaching the river crossing that led to Sodorrah. Balam was behind him, following with the food packs he had carried since the beginning. Because Ba'ar had not taken them off the night before, they were rubbing sores into Balam's skin. He had also picked up a stone in his hoof and walked with a limp. Ba'ar either did not notice or did not care. Ba'ar left the cover of the trees and walked to the riverbank and saw that the boats that normally ferried people from one side to the other had been burned. In the distance, he saw a glow beyond the trees as if a great fire were burning, and he thought he could hear screams.

However, Ba'ar was not concerned with what lay beyond the river. He was still pondering what Nabal had discussed with him that morning. Could he really rule Crespin? He did enjoy the idea of Sebastian and Bolo mucking his stalls and Shawndra fetching his food. But what of the Elder and Captain Hart? They would not serve him. Ba'ar figured there was an answer for that as well. They would have to share the same fate as anyone who did not serve him.

Balam whinnied and pulled at the reins and disturbed Ba'ar's fantasies of power. Ba'ar turned to chastise the horse only to find a large set of eyes glaring at him from the trees. "You should not leave the safety of the trees, young human," said the voice that matched the eyes. Ba'ar recognized it as the voice that quizzed him at the base of the mountain. The same eyes and voice that kept him from traveling with the others.

Ba'ar said, "I was looking for a way to cross. Had you been here earlier you would know that."

"I have been here for some time now," said Verdigris. "I have already scouted the shores and there is no way for us to cross. Now come with me. The rest of us are at the top of this bluff. Your presence is required by your captain."

Ba'ar thought to himself, *When I rule Crespin I will make sure I have a coat made of that animal's hide. No one will* require *me to do anything.*

He took Balam's reins and began leading him up the path to a high bluff where everyone had gathered. Everyone was there, including the four Baruk who had escorted them thus far. As Ba'ar led Balam into the camp, Bolo stepped forward and said, "The horse has a limp. I'll see to his hooves."

Ba'ar mumbled, "That's right, get in your practice for when you tend to my horses."

Shawndra said, "What did you say?"

"Nothing. Mind your own business. I know that's difficult for you," replied Ba'ar.

Ba'ar walked to the ledge where Sebastian, Captain Hart, and Lady Jeanine were standing and could see over the tree tops and all the way to Sodorrah. It looked as though half the city was on fire. "What is going on here?" asked Ba'ar in a commanding tone. Captain Hart gave Ba'ar a look that reminded him that he was only a ruler in his own mind, but in reality he was still a soldier and Captain Hart was still in command. Ba'ar changed his tone and said, "I mean, what are your orders, sir?"

Captain Hart said, "The city is in chaos, and we have to pass through it in order to find our way north. This won't be easy."

Lady Jeanine replied, "Not only that, but we have a responsibility to those that still live in Sodorrah to protect them. They are mainly fishermen who don't have the skill or the resolve for battle." Lady Jeanine called out to the Baruk, who were also gazing at the city as said, "What do your keen eyes see that can help us?"

Skiatook said, "The city was built with walls within walls. In the middle of the city is a watch tower. It seems as though the last of the townsfolk that have not been poisoned by the dead water are deep inside the last wall and taking refuge in the tower. They will not last long."

Shawndra said, "We must do something. Maybe we can storm the gates and help the townspeople get to safety."

Bolo had finished cleaning out Balam's hooves and had taken his packs off. He walked to the edge of the cliff and surveyed the city.

Ba'ar said, "We don't have the numbers for a siege. I say we bypass the city all together and let the people figure it out on their own. This whole situation is obviously of their own making."

"I think I would like another mind on the situation," said Lady Jeanine. She turned to Captain Hart and said, "I understand that young Bolo here has quite the mind for strategy. I wonder what his thoughts are on this situation?"

Ba'ar laughed and began saying, "Bolo? If we were talking about cooking and farming then I might think he had something useful to say, but this is not a task for—"

Ba'ar was interrupted by Sebastian who said excitedly, "Yes! Bolo has the best mind for this sort of thing. He knows how to get in and out of anywhere without being caught. Come on Bolo, tell us."

"Yes Bolo, speak up," said Captain Hart as he half asked and half ordered him.

"Well," said Bolo. "From what I can see, the walls are pretty thick and most of the people are in the city. If we can find a way to get the healthy people out and the sick people in at the same time, we can lock the gates and control the outer wall so that the sick people don't wander off into the mountains and hurt themselves."

Captain Hart scratched his chin and said, "Interesting. So rather than trying to fight the enemy out of an overrun city, we just use the city as a trap to keep them in?"

Ba'ar began to fidget with his hands as he realized that Bolo's plan just might work brilliantly. He had to find a flaw somewhere before Bolo was seen as something other than his future stable boy. "Well, how do you intend to get the townspeople out that have not been poisoned? Or do you wish to lock them up inside as well?

Shawndra said, "You have no room to talk, Ba'ar. You wanted to leave them all and pretend they don't exist."

Ba'ar turned to her and said, "Now you listen to me, you little—" Once again Ba'ar was cut off. This time by Lady Jeanine.

"The city has many wells in it. They feed into a cave that runs underneath the city. If we can enter the cave and find the well that feeds the innermost wall, then we can help the people escape through it," said Lady Jeanine.

Sebastian said, "But all the boats are burned, and we can't swim the river because the current would take us into the lake with the dead water?"

"There is more than one way to cross this river. If Mr. Bolo can pull off his part of the plan, then I'm sure I can get the people out."

"Well then," said Bolo. "Let's get started."

THE TORTAI

All of the group, including the Baruk, were standing in a circle looking down at a collection of rocks on a flat stone that had been arranged to look like the city. Lady Jeanine said, "Mr. Bolo, you have come up with a fine plan."

Bolo stood and straightened his back and said, "Thank you. Now, does everyone know their part?"

Captain Hart said, "Yes, Ba'ar and I will each ride a Baruk into the city and draw the poisoned townspeople deeper so that we can trap them inside."

Ba'ar interrupted, "Shouldn't we wait till dawn to do this?"

Captain Hart replied, "No, the night will keep them from knowing just how few we are. We will be able to keep the element of surprise longer."

Verdigris said, "Myself, Urune, and Bolo will shut the outer gates and lock them. Then all of us will patrol the outermost wall and keep everyone inside."

"Shutting the gates won't be easy since the infected people have blocked them open," replied Bolo.

Verdigris answered, "Don't worry about the gates, lad. Wood, steel, or stone will not stop us from fulfilling our task."

Sebastian said, "And I will go with Shawndra and Lady Jeanine under the city and get the healthy townspeople out through the well."

"And all of this is based on whether or not the Elder can get us across the river," said Ba'ar with a tone of contempt.

Oolagah, responded, "I know my part and I will do it, but I don't like the idea of carrying this one on my back. He has the stench of fear about him. And he wines like a wounded stag."

Ba'ar turned red with anger at the Baruk's comment. "I don't care to be around you either. I would much rather be on a trained war horse."

"Watch your tone, little man," said Urune. "That is my mate you are talking to, and I will not take your insults of her lightly."

Bolo spoke up, "I know this isn't the best plan to secure a city. But it's the best we can do with what we've got. Please Oolagah, just this once."

"I will carry him," said Oolagah as she nestled against Urune. "He will be safe with me. For now."

"Good, then it is settled," said Hart. "Let's get down to the river bank where the Elder will get us across." The Baruk gracefully and skillfully descended the cliff without a sound. Their human friends slid down the hill on the rocks and sand. All of the group approached the river bank, and the Elder stepped forward, lifted her arms, closed her eyes, and began to sing.

Bah-rah-key nap-she et Mai, wuhall tish-kuh-chee kah-all guh-moo-lah Has-so-lay-ahch luh-cahl chah woe nay key hah-rohphey luh-chahl-tah chahloo aychee Hago-ale mish-ah-chat chah-yehy chee hamuth chay tuh-ray chee hessed wuh-rah chameem. 103rd Song of Elders

When she had finished Ba'ar muttered, "I thought we had come here to cross the river, not hear a concert."

Lady Jeanine raised an eyebrow at him. "Ba'ar, I hear doubt in your voice. Instead of whispering them, why don't you step forward and bring your thoughts before everyone?"

Ba'ar's eyes narrowed as he squared his shoulders with the Elder and stepped forward to accept her challenge. "I don't see how so few with so little can take and hold an entire city. It is madness."

Bolo said, "If we use our assets in the proper way, we will be able to—"

Ba'ar interrupted, barely containing his anger. He couldn't bear the thought of Bolo being given preference over him, and now the young cadet had the gall to answer his question. "Assets! What assets? We are but three men at arms, two children and a...a..." Ba'ar was at a loss for a description when it came to the Elder.

Lady Jeanine turned her back on Ba'ar and looked to the river and said, "A what, Mr. Ba'ar?"

Ba'ar now had an opportunity to reveal his thoughts of the Elder fully to her. He stepped closer to her and leaned forward as if to hurl his words at her like spears. "You are an ancient relic from a bygone era. Your kind have disappeared, and you should have disappeared with them."

Sebastian had heard enough and stepped in between Ba'ar and Lady Jeanine. "You have done nothing but complain the entire time you have been on this journey. I think Verdigris was right when he said you only love yourself."

Ba'ar desperately wanted to teach this young boy a lesson in respect. But with Captain Hart close by and the Baruk near he knew not to make a move against him. However, the thought of disciplining Sebastian did cause a thin, wicked smile to snake across his face. Lady Jeanine thought that Ba'ar looked more like his father now more than ever.

Shawndra couldn't let an opportunity to speak her mind to Ba'ar pass. "You, as a soldier of the Citadel, are charged with the protection of all people of Crespin. You cannot abandon them."

Captain Hart finally stepped forward and said in a stern voice, "Enough. Ba'ar, you forget yourself. The Elder holds my respect and you will act as if she holds yours."

Ba'ar stepped close to Lady Jeanine and whispered so that only she could hear, "Just as long as you know, it is only an act."

Lady Jeanine replied back, "I know, you've been acting all your life." The two stepped away from each other. And Lady Jeanine walked over to the water and knelt by the edge. "This water is safe to drink. The current keeps the dead water from flowing up river," said Lady Jeanine as she reached her hand down and drank the ice cold water that came from the melted snow from deep in the mountains.

Sebastian asked, "That song you sang. It was the same healing song from when we were in Falls Lake. Is someone sick, and we just don't know it?"

Lady Jeanine replied, "The entire land of Crespin is sick from the dead water, but that is not what the song is for."

Shawndra had a puzzled look on her face. "But that song is for healing, even now I feel stronger for having heard it."

The Elder smiled, walked over to her, and said, "This is the living water in you listening to the song. For the rest of your days you will always feel this way when the ancient songs of the Elders are sung. But I did not sing for you this time. The water is much too cold for you to swim and the current would just wash you down river into the lake where the dead water will poison you. Building a boat would take too long, so we need some help."

Sebastian smiled and said, "You have a plan, don't you? You were calling someone to help us."

"There is no one left to call," said Ba'ar. "Unless your tune can dry up the waters, it is useless to us."

Lady Jeanine turned from the group and looked out over the water, drew her sword, and held it out, "We will pass over the water." A great rush of water was heard and from the dark depths of the river arose several giant shells that were over twenty hands high. Legs sprouted out from underneath them as they came into the shallows at the edge of the river. A giant head came snaking out the front of each shell, and as they exhaled, the mists from their noses came out with such a force that everyone but the Baruk had to take a step back. Their eyes were deep green, and one opened its mouth and spoke with a moan, "Um, ah, we heard the song of the ancients and have come to aid the servant of Mai."

Lady Jeanine turned back to her group and said, "Behold, the great Tortai."

Shawndra's mouth gaped open as her curiosity made her walk up to the Tortai and place her hands on the wet shell. "These are amazing. I've never even heard of them," she said in a half whisper.

Lady Jeanine faced the Tortai and said, "Great masters of the water, we need your strength to carry us to the west side of the river."

The Tortai that spoke before said, "Um, ah, the Great Mai gathered us in this river many moons ago so that we may assist his servants in the days of cleansing. We will take you where you need to go."

Sebastian smiled so big that his face could barely contain it. The secrets of Crespin and the Elders were wonderful indeed. Bolo did not move, except to steady himself and keep from falling over. Everyone else seemed genuinely impressed, even Ba'ar.

Lady Jeanine said, "Quickly, everyone climb on their backs. Sebastian and Shawndra, you are with me on this one. Skiatook, please see to it that Balam gets on with you. Keep him from falling in." Everyone, even the Baruk, did as she said, and the powerful legs of the Tortai pushed them out into the depths of the river. The water covered the legs and head of the Tortai, but everyone stayed dry riding on their backs.

Bolo called out to the Elder, "How long can they stay under the water like that?"

Lady Jeanine answered back, "They don't have to come up for air for days."

Captain Hart said in a low but clear voice, "No more calling out to each other. We are getting close to the city, and there may be scouts on the banks."

Lady Jeanine leaned over toward the water and whispered, "Now old friend, take me to the cave that feeds the wells under the city." Immediately the Tortai that she, Sebastian, and Shawndra were riding changed course and with surprising speed began making its way upriver. They were soon gone from Captain Hart's sight as a veil of night covered them.

"I can't see them anymore," said Bolo.

"I can," said Verdigris. "They are headed for a cave upriver."

Oolagah said, "The river banks are clear of onlookers. There is a dock straight ahead, but it has not been maintained for some time."

"Good," said Captain Hart. "That is where we will make our landing and then proceed to the city of Sodorrah."

As the Tortai swam up alongside the docks, everyone jumped off their backs and on to the wood planks that popped and squeaked under their feet. Skiatook lifted Balam in his mighty jaws and placed the horse on the pier. The same jaws had torn apart many a wild stag and carried it over the mountains to the home of the Baruk. Now they were gentle and carried the horse without leaving a mark. Without waiting for thanks or giving a word of advice, the Tortai drifted back out to the river depths and then sank below the water out of sight.

Bolo said, "I don't imagine anyone at the Citadel has ever had a boat ride quite like that."

Captain Hart ran swiftly without making a noise to the wood's edge and found the trail. He motioned for everyone to come to him. "I need one of the Baruk to scout ahead and let me know if there is anyone on the trail. We will stop as close to the gates as we can without being seen."

Urune said, "I will go." Only the rush of wind

could be heard as the powerful Baruk disappeared into the darkness.

Skiatook, Verdigris, and Oolagah lowered themselves to the ground, and Verdigris said, "It is better if you three get on our backs. The journey will be faster and safer." Captain Hart and Bolo quickly climbed on the Baruk, but Ba'ar stood beside Oolagah and said, "How are you supposed to ride this thing? There is no saddle."

Bolo replied, "Just grab onto some fur and hang on. Oolagah will make sure you don't fall off."

Ba'ar didn't like it that Bolo was giving him riding lessons. He grabbed a handful of hair and swung himself onto the Baruk's back. He then raised his heels to kick the sides as if he were riding a horse when Oolagah turned her head quickly and said with a deep and dangerous growl, "I'm not some pack animal. I go when I please and not a moment sooner." Ba'ar lowered his heels and held on tight as Oolagah leaped into the night, followed by the rest of the Baruk and their riders.

The Tortai carrying Lady Jeanine, Shawndra, and Sebastian took them to a cave opening at the edge of the river. The Tortai raised his head above water and said, "Um, ah, this is as far as I can go. The cave is too small for me to fit, you must travel from here alone.

All three riders slid off the Tortai's shell and into the knee deep water. Lady Jeanine said, "You have honored us and Mai with your service. Go and rejoin your kind." The Tortai slid backwards into the deep waters of the river and disappeared.

Sebastian said, "Too bad he couldn't go with us into the cave. I bet he would be useful."

Shawndra answered, "Tortai or not, let's get on with it." She turned and stepped into the entrance to the cave. The only light that could be seen came from somewhere deep inside. It illuminated a path cut into the stone that followed a stream deep into the cave. The path also led downriver next to the river bank.

Lady Jeanine pointed to the path and said, "This path was cut into the stone many years ago when the city was built. If we stay on it, we will find our way to the innermost wells of the city. It will also be the way we will lead the people out of here and to safety. We must move swiftly if we are to keep pace with Captain Hart and the others." Upon saying this, all three picked up their pace and began to make their way into the cave.

Captain Hart and the rest of his group had arrived at the clearing outside of the gates of Sodorrah. The outermost wall was high, but the parapets were empty. The only guards to speak of were crazed villagers wandering to and from the lake's edge. The Baruk and their riders gathered out of sight, and Captain Hart started to speak when Skiatook said, "Quiet, get down!" The Baruk lowered themselves to the ground, and Captain Hart, Bolo, and Ba'ar slid off their backs. Even Balam seemed to try to hide himself behind a tree. Skiatook continued, "A group of villagers are coming out."

Fifteen villagers, all infected by the dead water, ran out of the city of Sodorrah carrying four villagers that were fighting against them. They had not yet tasted the dead water and still had their wits about them. The infected villagers dragged them to the lake's edge and forced them into the water and held them down until they drank the dead water. It didn't take long until the healthy villagers were convulsing and shaking on the sandy banks, rolling and writhing in pain. Bolo said, "I've never seen anything like that. How can a person get so sick that they would do that to their kinsman?" No one answered because no one knew.

At the entrance to the city, Ba'ar spied something familiar. A shadowy figure was lurking about and directing the actions of those under the influence of the dead water. It was Nabal, the oily companion he had met on the road. Nabal was enjoying the sight and had apparently led the siege of this fishing city. Ba'ar remembered that Nabal had offered to make him a prince in Crespin if he would join him. It seemed that his offer was not as empty as Ba'ar had assumed. Nabal stepped back into the city, followed by the crazed townsfolk that were doing his bidding.

Captain Hart kept his eyes on the villagers that were lying on the bank. Before he went into the city, he needed to know if the people on the beach would be a threat.

Skiatook said, "It should not take long for the dead water to run its course. However, if we tarry here too much longer there will be few people left for my little brother Sebastian to save."

"I agree," said the captain. Hart turned to Bolo and Ba'ar and said, "Ba'ar, we will draw the townspeople deep into the city so that Bolo and the other Baruk can shut the gates. Do not use your sword for combat unless you have to."

"I understand," said Ba'ar.

"Do you?" said Oolagah. "I smell deception in the air."

"Ba'ar will do as he is ordered," said Captain Hart. "Now, let's ride swiftly and do what we can to save the city."

———

Lady Jeanine led Sebastian and Shawndra along the path that led deeper into the city. They walked under three sets of arches that Lady Jeanine said were the foundations of the three walls that made up the city of Sodorrah. At the end of the cave was a faint beam of light that came from a hole in the roof of the cavern. A rope hung halfway down with a bucket attached to it. "This is the final well that leads to the innermost chamber of the city. We will be able to get the people out this way."

Sebastian began looking around and then saw

Shawndra doing the same. They had realized that the cave was over fifty feet high and they had nothing to climb up with. Sebastian put his hands on the walls and noticed that they were very slick and very slimy. He looked at the Elder and said, "Um, I beg your pardon, but how are we going to get up there?"

Lady Jeanine closed her eyes, faced the pool of water and began to sing.

Lahmnazsay-chahl-shoshahn-neem   luh-dah-weed hoshee-aynee eloheem kee vah-oo mahyeem chath-nah-phesh, Taaba tiy biyween mtsuwlaah weeyn maa Baattiy b'ma maqeey-mayim wshibolet sh'Taapaatniy. 69th Song of the Elders

As she finished a great rush of water could be heard and the water began to swirl, froth, and rise. Lady Jeanine took both Sebastian and Shawndra by the hand and said, "Quickly now, jump into the water."

Shawndra said, "What? I don't know. What is happening?"

Lady Jeanine said, "No time for questions, just trust me." All three of them jumped at the same time and as soon as they went into the water, it sprayed them through the well and out of the cavern into the city. It looked as though the earth had spit them out.

When they landed, Sebastian scrambled quickly to get to his feet and shouted with a large grin on his face, "That was amazing! We have got to do that again."

However, the look on Shawndra's face as she sneezed the water out of her nose let Sebastian know that she was less than pleased. She said, "No, let's not do that again. Next time let's just remember to bring a ladder."

Lady Jeanine was now on her feet and said, "Get up quickly, Shawndra. We are being watched." As Sebastian and Shawndra looked around, they realized that they had landed in the middle of the courtyard of the innermost wall of the city and were surrounded by the last inhabitants of Sodorrah that had not succumbed to the dead water.

Sebastian stepped forward toward the nearest man, who cowered away from him instantly. "Wait," said Sebastian. "We're not here to hurt you; we want to help you escape."

"And why should we believe you?" asked a man who stepped out from the crowd. "Our own kinsman have been poisoned and turned against us. And I don't know you." The man then raised a gigging pole used to spear fish and pointed it at Sebastian. "Tell me why we shouldn't just toss you over the wall to those crazies on the other side?"

"Because I know you," said Lady Jeanine. "And you know me, Mr. Rowland. You were the apprentice to Jeroboam and you helped me get Cakal Corvin's son out of Falls Lake before the dead water killed the city."

The man leaned forward with surprise and said, "How do you know about that day? Nearly all the witnesses to that day perished. I helped Lady Jeanine, the Elder. She was ancient thirteen years ago. You could not be her unless…unless you have renewed yourself for the journey of cleansing."

The Elder stepped closer to him and said, "Rowland, I sent you here thirteen years ago so that you could hold this city from plunging into the darkness of the dead water for as long as you could. And now I have returned, and this young lad that you are pointing your weapon towards is the hope of us all."

The man dropped his gigging pole and fell to the ground weeping and cried out, "I am Rowland, apprentice to Jeroboam, and I am at the service of the last Elder."

The townsfolk that had all witnessed these events all dropped their crude weapons as well and walked toward Lady Jeanine, Sebastian, and Shawndra and began to ask, "Are you here to rescue us? How will we get out? Will we be able to cure our loved ones on the other side of this wall?"

Lady Jeanine motioned for silence and said, "Rowland, your time has come again to serve the Elders. You will take your tallest ladder, put it in the well, and escape from underneath the city. Soldiers of the Citadel will lure the sick townspeople deeper into the city where we can then shut the gates and trap them inside until the dead water can be cleansed."

Rowland replied, "Yes my lady, we will all do as you ask." With a few quick commands to the people, Rowland had them all scurrying about gathering everything they would need to evacuate the city.

Sebastian smiled at his Elder, and she smiled

back. Then Sebastian saw something alarming at the edge of her young face. Her hair was beginning to turn gray again.

———•———

Captain Hart was riding Skiatook, and Ba'ar was riding Oolagah. Bolo had slid off Verdigris' back and was holding Balam's reins. Captain Hart said, "Ba'ar and I will ride with Oolagah and Skiatook into the city and get the infected townspeople to follow us. When we get to the most inner wall, the Baruk will jump clear to the top, and then we will make sure the poisoned townsfolk cannot get out and hurt themselves."

Bolo said, "And I will go with Urune and Verdigris to free up the gates to close them. I'll tie up the horse here so he will be out of danger."

"Very good," said Captain Hart. "Are you ready, Ba'ar?" Ba'ar was distracted by the presence of Nabal in the city and the possibilities that it would mean. He didn't even hear the question his captain had asked. "Ba'ar, I asked if you are ready."

"Oh, yes, Captain," said Ba'ar with a start. "I'm ready if this Baruk is."

Urune said with a snort, "If you mistreat her, little man, you will answer to me."

Ba'ar didn't even pay attention to the Baruk's comments. He got a good hold onto her fur and said, "Let's go." Oolagah and Skiatook both bolted for the city gates. They were fast and fearless as they leaped over the sickened people at the entrance.

Immediately they were followed into the city as people saw them run past. The Baruk and their riders leaped over boxes and around corners as they weaved their way through the streets.

Captain Hart called out, "Let's split up, we can lead more people toward the center of the city that way."

"Agreed," said Skiatook. At the next corner Oolagah turned a sharp left, and Skiatook leaped over a barricade to go straight. They were now circling toward each other from different directions within the city.

Oolagah said, "Only two more turns left before we meet at the center, try not to fall off." As she said this, a spear struck her in her hip, and she fell to the ground and threw Ba'ar through the air. After landing, he rolled over many times.

Ba'ar got up and shook the dust off himself and said, "Try not to fall off, huh. That was your fault."

Oolagah got up but was dragging her back leg behind her. "I will not be able to carry you any farther. However, use that ladder on the ground next to that pole to climb up to the top of the wall."

Ba'ar ran over and picked up the ladder. He could hear the sound of the screeching townspeople getting closer. Ba'ar said, "What about you? You are too heavy for this ladder."

Oolagah said, "Carry that axe up with you, when you are at the top, cut that pole there in half, and I will be able to climb up it."

Ba'ar grabbed the axe and climbed the ladder as swiftly as he could. As soon as he was on top, he ran over to the pole and raised the axe to cut it down. Then, out of the corner of his eye, he saw Nabal. Nabal had a sinister grin and was shaking his head. He didn't want Ba'ar to provide a way for the Baruk to get out. Ba'ar knew that if he did not help the Baruk, if he left Oolagah to the crowd, he would be labeled a traitor and a coward. But if the Baruk died, then maybe he could keep all the glory for himself, and he would be praised by his captain for succeeding by himself. And maybe he could even join Nabal and take the city for himself. The temptation was just too tasty for Ba'ar to pass up.

"What are you waiting for?" cried Oolagah. "Cut down the pole, so I can climb out."

Ba'ar muttered under his breath, "You don't give me orders." He then dropped the axe to the ground and turned away from Oolagah.

The crazed townspeople finally caught up with the wounded Baruk and surrounded her. She snapped and howled and snarled and did what she could to keep them away from her. But it was just a matter of time before her wounds made her too weak to fight back.

As Ba'ar made his way back to the outer wall so that he could rejoin his group as a hero, he began rehearsing in his mind the different stories he could tell. He would say how Oolagah had fought bravely, but in the end she was overtaken. Ba'ar would tell them how he stayed as long as he could to defend her corpse, but ultimately he had to retreat so that the city could be saved. He smiled as he heard the howls of the Baruk behind him. He knew it wouldn't be long until she was silenced.

———•———

As the last villager climbed down the ladder into the well, Lady Jeanine and Sebastian heard the shrill howl of an injured Baruk. Sebastian turned quickly and said, "That sounded like Oolagah." Both Sebastian and the Elder looked to the top of the wall and saw Ba'ar standing on the edge, looking down the other side, with an axe raised high in the air preparing to cut down a pole. He then dropped the axe and turned and ran away. Again Oolagah could be heard, but this time she was snarling and fighting.

Sebastian said, "It sounds like she's in trouble."

"I agree," said the Elder. "Come over here next to these stacks of wood. You can climb them to the top of the wall."

Sebastian did as she asked and quickly made his way to the top of the innermost wall. He looked down on the other side and was shocked to see Oolagah snapping and snarling to keep the sickened villagers at a distance. Her hip had been injured, and she was not able to leap away. Sebastian saw one man in the back find a spear and started running at Oolagah while she was facing the opposite direction. Sebastian looked around desperately, found a loose rock, pried it from the wall, and flung it at the man carrying the spear. The rock struck the crazed man in the chest as he was only a few feet from delivering a fatal blow to Oolagah. He dropped the spear and cried out in pain as he ran away. Oolagah turned and saw the spear on the ground and the hurt man and looked up to Sebastian.

Sebastian yelled, "How can I help you?"

Oolagah said, "Cut that pole down and I can climb up."

Sebastian picked up the axe Ba'ar had dropped and began hacking on it. It only took a few swings before it began popping and splintering as it fell over. Oolagah dug her claws into it and climbed to safety on top of the wall with Sebastian. "Where is that coward you call Ba'ar?" she demanded.

"Did he leave you here?" asked Sebastian.

Oolagah said, "Death holds no power over a Baruk. If my life was required, then to die would be gain. However, he ran from battle and left another to die. That is without excuse." Oolagah tried to take a step and winced in pain. Her hip had been pierced, and she had lost a lot of blood.

Sebastian saw the wound and called out to Lady Jeanine, "Oolagah is wounded. She needs help."

The Elder replied, "Go with her and make your way to the outer wall. Find Captain Hart and tell him all that you have learned. I will bring these villagers to the gates by way of the river pass." Lady Jeanine walked over to the well and disappeared down the ladder.

"Come on, I'll go with you to the gates," said Sebastian to Oolagah.

Oolagah replied, "Yes, I look forward to seeing Ba'ar receive his punishment for his treachery. As for you, young Sebastian, I look forward to seeing you get your reward."

The Traitor Revealed

Bolo took Balam's reins and tied him to a small sapling. He figured that would be good enough to hold the horse for now. As soon as the sickened townspeople had followed Captain Hart, Ba'ar, Ski-atook, and Oolagah into the city, Bolo, Verdigris, and Urune rushed the gates to close them. They had been kept open by poles propped against the doors and sand piled in front of them. Urune and Verdigris began digging feverishly to remove the sand and Bolo started knocking down the poles. Bolo was so focused on what he was doing that he stopped paying attention to the townspeople that had been dragged into the dead water and were lying on the shore. They had woken up, and the dead water had taken hold of their minds. Upon seeing Bolo and the two Baruk, they began to rush them. Bolo heard the thumping of feet on the sand and turned just before the people were on top of him. He didn't have time to draw his sword or call out for help. However, just before they seized him, they were hit by a horse in full gallop. All four of the people flew through the air and landed in varying positions. Fortunately for Bolo, Balam was stronger than the small tree he had tied him to and Balam pulled it out of the ground when he saw the people get up and run at him.

"Well, that beats all I've ever seen," said Bolo. He turned to the Baruk and said, "Did you see that?"

"Yes," said Verdigris. "You were saved by a horse. Congratulations." Verdigris seemed uninterested in Bolo's amazement.

Urune said, "Maybe you would like to celebrate later. We still have a gate to close."

Bolo nodded and smiled, "That's right, but old Balam here has proven he's good for more than just carrying food." Bolo took some rope and tied Balam to one of the larger poles and said, "Now, let's put you to work, old friend." Balam snorted and pawed at the ground as he pulled the poles from the door. After running the last of the poisoned townsfolk into the city, it wasn't long before Bolo and the Baruk were able to push the door closed and then put the poles back in place to prop the door shut.

"Well, that ought to hold'em," said Bolo.

Verdigris said, "We should know any moment how everyone else fared." Even as he said that Ski-atook, who was carrying Captain Hart, leaped off the top of the wall and then trotted over to the gates.

"Good job with the gates. Have we heard from Ba'ar or the Elder?"

"Not yet," said Bolo. "I'm sure they'll be along directly."

Lady Jeanine and Shawndra walked out of the woods followed by Rowland and the remainder of the townsfolk who were not poisoned. Captain Hart dismounted Skiatook and said, "Where is Sebastian?"

Lady Jeanine replied, "He will be here soon. He has much to tell you."

Urune said, "The whiner and Oolagah should have returned by now."

Captain Hart said, "It might have taken them longer to get out of the city. Jumping from wall to wall was getting tricky."

A voice was heard from on top of the wall as all of the group at the gate looked up and saw Ba'ar waving at them. "How do I get down from here?" he yelled.

Urune said, "You come down with Oolagah."

Ba'ar replied, "She did not make it."

His words struck them all very hard. Immediately Urune got a running start and leaped to the top of the wall and put himself squarely in front of Ba'ar. "What do you mean? How does a Baruk not survive and a man does? What did you do?"

Captain Hart called to Urune, "Bring him here. We need to question him."

Urune answered back, "I do not answer to any man. I will question him here."

Skiatook said, "Urune, you answer to me. Bring the man to us, and we will all have a chance to hear the truth." Urune bared his teeth to Ba'ar and bristled his thick mane, but in the end, he did as he was told. But he did not allow Ba'ar to ride on his back. He scooped him up in his mouth and then jumped off the ledge. Ba'ar was heard screaming the entire time, even when Urune spat him onto the ground.

Captain Hart said, "Everyone back off." He then stepped closer to Ba'ar as he brushed the dirt off his clothing. "What happened in the city?"

Ba'ar straightened himself and said, "Myself and Oolagah rode into the city, this you know. After we went separate ways, Oolagah was injured and I was thrown from her back. I stayed and fought with her until we were overwhelmed by the people inside the city. I stayed with her as long as I could, but in the end, they were just too much for her. I'm sorry, Urune, but your mate is gone."

Urune lifted his gaze to the night sky and let out a painful howl that was the most bitter mix of sorrow any had ever heard. Captain Hart said to Ba'ar, "I'm sure you did your best to save her."

"No, he didn't!" came a voice from the edge of the darkness. Coming into view was Sebastian and Oolagah. "We found a way down on the far side of the city. We've been trying to get back here as fast as Oolagah can travel."

Lady Jeanine quickly went to her side and found her wound. "The injury is deep, but not fatal. We will need to go to the forest to find healing roots."

Urune went to Oolagah and said, "The one called Ba'ar said you were killed, and it almost killed me."

Oolagah said, "The one called Ba'ar is a liar."

Captain Hart looked at Ba'ar who had turned as pale as the mist. "Tell me again what happened. But this time, tell me the truth."

"I, uh, what I mean is, I'm not sure." For the first time Ba'ar was without witty or snide comeback. There was no slight of hand to play. No deception could cover over the truth of the moment. He had lied and run.

Captain Hart stood squarely in front of Ba'ar and growled, "Answer me, soldier!"

Oolagah spoke up, "I was injured and Ba'ar climbed to safety and was supposed to cut a timber down so that I could get away as well. But he deliberately left me to die at the hands of the mob, ran from battle, and lied to you. It was Sebastian that came to my rescue. It is he that saved my life."

Captain Hart looked at Lady Jeanine and asked, "Is this true?"

Lady Jeanine replied, "It is as they say."

Captain Hart looked back to Ba'ar and said, "What do you have to say in your defense? What can you possibly say to explain your actions?"

Ba'ar stepped backwards and his frown began to quiver. His face was flushed, and his eyes seemed to search the ground for some fitting answer written in the sand. "I did leave this animal. But only because her purpose had been completed. She took me deep inside the city, and once she was injured, she was of no more use." Ba'ar began to speak louder and thump his chest in a mixture of anger, fear, and panic. "I've done everything asked of me. I've put up with these children, I've held my tongue with this washed up Elder and ignored all of the failings of Bolo, who should never have been a soldier to begin with." Then Ba'ar said something that made everyone gasp. "I've even followed your overly sentimental commands. You are so concerned with not hurting people that you won't do what is necessary to win a war. If only you would—" Ba'ar never got to finish his sentence.

Captain Hart, for the first time on the journey, raised his voice. He yelled, "Silence!" Hart's command stole the breath from Ba'ar's lungs. Even the Baruk seemed to shudder at the command. "I've heard enough of your complaints and excuses. I've excused your rotten attitude for years thinking that I could train it out of you. But I've come to realize over the past couple of days that you are just cruel. You have a mean streak in you that you enjoy, and your pride will not allow you to face it." Captain Hart took a couple of steps away from Ba'ar and regained his composure and looked him in the eye. "Ba'ar, son of Halal, as Captain of the guard of the Citadel, you are charged with deserting a comrade in arms and running from battle. For these things, I relieve you of your rank. I am ordering you to return to the city of Falls Lake and surrender your sword and blade. You are hereby expelled from being a soldier."

Sebastian and Shawndra were speechless. They could never have seen such a turn of events. Ba'ar began to walk backward away from the group. Captain Hart continued, "You may stay with the city of Sodorrah until the dead water is cleansed. But you may not give any orders, for you no longer have any authority."

Ba'ar looked up from the ground and said, "You are not my captain anymore. And you may not give me any orders either. You will regret this. You will look back on this day and remember it as the day you made your greatest mistake." After saying this, Ba'ar ran into the darkness and disappeared.

The rest of the townspeople that had been saved had come out of the woods and were being led by Rowland. "What are we to do now?" he asked.

Captain Hart said, "Bolo, come here."

Bolo stepped quickly. After witnessing Ba'ar being dismissed, he didn't want to give Captain Hart any reason to dismiss him. "Yes sir, what would you have me do?"

Captain Hart continued, "Bolo, I am placing you in charge of the defense of this city. It was your plan that saved the people, and so you will stay here as the rest of us travel upstream. Do you understand?"

"I, I'm not sure sir," stammered Bolo.

Captain Hart softened his tone and placed his hand on Bolo's shoulder. "You've done well today.

You've earned this. You will keep those in the city safe until the living water flows. You will have the help of the Baruk and what townspeople are left. This is very important. The people don't have the training for such a task. You do. Will you accept?"

Bolo swelled with joy as he excitedly saluted and said, "Yes sir, yes sir, I will accept."

Captain Hart turned to Skiatook and said, "Will you and the rest of your clan stay here and help Bolo hold the city?"

Skiatook said, "We will not be able to travel until Oolagah is better healed. So yes, we will stay."

Finally, Captain Hart turned to Oolagah and Urune. "I ask you not to seek revenge on Ba'ar. I am asking you to let him live."

Urune replied, "To let him live with his shame and treachery is more cruel than death. I would have had compassion on him and ended his suffering. I will honor your request."

Lady Jeanine finally spoke, "It seems that for now all is settled. Debts are reckoned, and the unworthy are expelled." The Elder turned to Sebastian, placed her hand on his shoulder and smiled sweetly as she said, "I am especially proud of you, Sebastian. You are a true hero."

The Elder then brushed the hair from her face and turned her gaze upriver and said, "Let's turn our thoughts to the end of our journey. We must make final preparations to go to the cave of the source. We will leave at first light tomorrow."

AN UNEXPECTED FIND

"I am the Great Mai, and I beckon you to come!" Sebastian awoke with a jerk. The voice he had heard in his dream echoed through his mind. His eyes were still filled with sleep. Everything was hazy and blurred as he tried to clear his sight. The sun had not yet risen, and everyone was still sleeping, everyone but Lady Jeanine. She was huddled close to the remaining heat in the glowing embers of their pitiful little fire. Her skin was pale, and she didn't look well.

Sebastian sat up and spoke to her in a hushed voice, "My lady, have you slept at all?" His words almost seemed to startle her. She seemed to search the darkness to find him, and once she did she had difficulty holding his gaze.

"My strength is fading, Sebastian," said Lady Jeanine. "Soon I will lose my youthful appearance, and I will no longer have the strength of the Elders. I just hope I can hold on long enough to make it to the cave."

Sebastian shuffled over to his beloved Elder and took her hand in his. For the first time her hands were cold. "Don't say such things. You are the strongest of all creatures. Of course you will make it."

Jeanine gave Sebastian a smile, but he was worried because her eyes no longer looked vibrant and alive. They almost seemed hollow. She said, "If I fall, make sure you continue on. Don't waste any time in empty ritual. As long as the dead water flows, all of Crespin is dying."

Sebastian put his arm around Lady Jeanine, and she leaned over and put her head on his shoulder. She continued, "Just a little way up this path is the entrance to the cave. You will stay close to Captain Hart. Shawndra will help me."

"I will not leave you," said Sebastian. Ordinarily such defiance might bring a harsh look or a quick correction from the Elder. However, this time she gave a weak smile and said, "I know your heart, Sebastian. You are like a son to me. I know you want to protect me, but you must honor me by doing what I tell you to do. Somehow, all that we have done, all that we are going to do depends on you. I am certain of this."

Sebastian's eyes narrowed as he struggled to understand. He was searching the red embers of the fire in front of him as if they would reveal some secret that would make everything make sense. "Why me? I don't understand."

Lady Jeanine sat back up and put her hand on Sebastian's back and said, "The ways of Mai are not always clear, but they don't remain unclear forever. All will be revealed soon. In fact, the sooner we get moving, the sooner we will know the end of our story."

"And then we will be able to go home and have an end to this terrible time," said Sebastian.

Lady Jeanine smiled again and said, "Or maybe we will understand that all of this was just a new beginning."

A large grin spread across Sebastian's face as he said, "Now that sounds like the words of an Elder. All that talk of not making it was worrying me."

Shawndra raised herself up from her uncomfortable spot near the fire and stretched as she said in a small crackling voice, "Who was worried?"

The Elder replied, "No one child. Wake Captain Hart and load everything on the horse. It's time to finish our journey."

The tired dwindling group packed up their camp and loaded Balam and began the last of their journey. They would be at the cave of the source by the time the noonday sun was at its zenith.

The dead water was now a thick ooze and made a sound like a wet blanket being slapped against rocks as it flowed downstream. There was no life sprouting from the cracks in the rocks and no vines or branches that hung over the stream. Fragile life had no chance this close to the dead water.

Captain Hart was in the lead with Sebastian behind him holding onto Balam's reins. Shawndra had been walking with Lady Jeanine, and she had noticed that the Elder's weight on her shoulder was increasing with every turn of the path. Jeanine's hands were becoming spotty and her hair was beginning to streak gray. Shawndra said, "If we take Balam's packs off, you can ride the horse, I mean, if you need to."

The Elder squeezed Shawndra's shoulder gently and said, "When I am not strong enough to carry myself, then my journey will be over." The look of determination in the Elder's eye told Shawndra not to press the Elder with help.

Captain Hart signaled everyone to stop. He was studying something on the other side of a large rock. He called out for the Elder and said, "Lady Jeanine, you need to see this."

Shawndra led the Elder to stand beside Captain Hart, and they all looked behind the rock to see a human skeleton laid out on the ground. The bones were many years old and had turned grey from being so close to the dead water. However, the reason the Captain wanted the Elder to examine them is because of the robe that was lying nearby. Whoever this was wore the robe of an Elder's apprentice.

Lady Jeanine examined the find carefully, and Sebastian was surprised to see a single tear roll down her face. "Lady Jeanine, do you know who this is?" asked Sebastian.

"Yes," replied the Elder. "This was my apprentice, Aswan. I sent her here to undergo the test of the Elders more than thirteen years ago. She never returned."

Shawndra asked, "How do you know it's her?"

Lady Jeanine responded, "I made her this robe. She was the best of us."

Captain Hart asked, "If it was more than thirteen years ago then it wasn't the dead water that killed her. Maybe she fell or became ill?"

Lady Jeanine's face showed her disbelief at the thought. "This young lady was well trained. She was healthy and well skilled. Look there," Lady Jeanine pointed to a hole in the back of the skull. "She had been hit by something. You don't get that serious an injury from falling down. What's more, the fatal hit came from behind, so whoever did this knew her well enough for her to turn her back on them."

Captain Hart readjusted his sword belt and armor and said, "I'd like to believe that because this happened so long ago that there is no danger to us now. However, something tells me that we are in danger here."

"Yes, I agree," said the Elder. "Aswan's standard is missing. Whoever attacked her took it. It isn't valuable to anyone who isn't traveling to the cave of the source. The puzzle is beginning to fit together now."

"What is it?" asked Sebastian. "You know who did this. Please tell us."

"I don't know anything for certain. However, we need to be on our guard, now more than ever." Lady Jeanine put her hand back on Shawndra's shoulder and said, "The cave is not far. Let's get moving and face whatever is waiting for us."

Sebastian took Balam's reins, and Captain Hart took the lead again. Within just a few turns on the winding path, they would find the answers they were looking for.

THE CAVE OF THE SOURCE

Around the final turn of the rapidly narrowing path was the entrance to the cave of the source. There were no ornate carvings or banners to show the importance of such a place. Only an oily thick ooze that flowed out the mountain. The path was too narrow to lead a horse so Sebastian tied Balam's reins to a dead stump that once was a tree growing from a crack in the rock.

Captain Hart said, "Check your weapons. If there is a threat to us, we will meet it in the cave."

Sebastian removed three torches from Balam's packs that he had collected at Sodorrah. With his flint, he set fire to them and handed one to Captain Hart, another to Shawndra, and one for himself. Lady Jeanine was barely able to carry herself.

"I will go first," said Captain Hart. "Sebastian, you

follow me, and keep that dagger ready. Shawndra, if you have to, use the Elder's sword. Now, let's get going.

The captain walked confidently into the cave as the light from his torch pushed back the darkness. The tunnel was so narrow that they had to straddle the dead water to get by. Sebastian had been taught all his life to stay as far from the liquid death as possible. Now he was as close as anyone could get without actually stepping into it.

The narrow tunnel opened to a larger cave where a thick ooze could be heard glopping down a rocky slope, the sound that mud makes when it falls to the ground. Lady Jeanine took Shawndra's torch and held her flame high and a pale light began reflecting off the dim crystals that were covered over with an oily slime that came from years of close proximity to the polluted water. Sebastian could tell that once this room had been a great cathedral with natural gems that hung from the ceiling and formed from the floor. Stalactites and stalagmites made of clear and multicolored crystals that could radiate light were now dirty and smudged with dead water.

"This was once beautiful and inspiring," said the Lady. "When I traveled here to become an Elder and drink from the spring, this cave had a light of its own. It is sad to see such a beautiful place stained by death." Jeanine steadied herself against the rock wall on one side of her and Shawndra on the other.

"It could use a good scrubbing," said Shawndra. "If I had a month I couldn't get this place clean."

"Don't worry, my dear girl," said the Lady. "Once the living water flows, the mess will take care if itself." Jeanine was trying to be reassuring, but something in her was unsettled. Sebastian felt it too.

"I feel like there are eyes looking upon us," said Sebastian.

"Yes, I feel it too," said Captain Hart. He drew his sword slowly and took a defensive place in front of the small group.

"A fine group we make," said Sebastian. "Only half of us know how to use weapons, and only one of us is able. Maybe we should turn back and get help from Bolo."

Hart turned and kneeled to look Sebastian in the eye, "Mr. Bolo has his own problems, and we can't leave the good people of Sodorrah to fend for themselves. But your best weapon of all, the one that I need you to use right now is your courage." Hart put his hand on Sebastian's shoulder and also looked at Shawndra. "When Ba'ar betrayed Oolagah in battle, he was fully armed. But you were faithful." Hart looked at Shawndra, "Both of you were faithful. Use the weapons you know, and we will be just fine."

"Wise words, Captain," said Lady Jeanine with a weak smile.

"I'll do my best, Captain," said Sebastian as he straightened under the weight of Captain Hart's arm. "Now, let's see what's at the top of this rock."

"Yes, let's!" said Shawndra

The waterfall fell from the top of a rock structure

that climbed close to the roof of the cave. It looked like a giant altar with a bowl shaped pool at the top with black sludge that seemed to vomit itself over the edge. Sebastian could see the top dimly.

Captain Hart led the group up the rock formation from which the spoiled water flowed. He had handed his torch over to Sebastian so that he would have both hands free. His sword was drawn, and he hid his short blade from view under his cloak. He wanted to be ready to defend with one hand while striking with his other. Lady Jeanine was having difficulty walking up the steep incline. Sebastian and Shawndra were helping her walk as her strength was leaving. When Hart reached the top, he called for a torch.

"Give me a torch," said Hart, as he sheathed his short blade. "I need to see what's up here." Sebastian passed him a torch, and the captain held it out over the top of the cauldron. He saw a pool of pure sludge that was flowing over the edge. "Where is the source of the spring? Is it under the pool?" Hart called to Jeanine.

"No," said Lady Jeanine. "The source of the spring is in the wall toward the back of this pool. We have to walk around the edge and see what is the problem. Whatever you do, do not get any of the dead water on you. It is very concentrated here because it is so close to the source. Just a few drops can weaken you so that you can't defend yourself. More than that and it can be fatal." Lady Jeanine's hope was beginning to leave her with her strength.

She had hoped to find what was polluting the stream before they reached this point. What if it really was the living water itself that had turned dark and poisonous? What if the problem was deep within the mountain where they could not reach? If that was the problem, then all of their work was for nothing and Crespin would be dead forever.

"Look!" shouted Sebastian. "Against the back wall, do you see it, Captain?" Sebastian was pointing to a huddled mass on the back side of the pool. It was dark and oily but it moved ever so slightly.

"Yes, I see it, whatever it is. Shawndra, you stay with the lady. Sebastian, you come with me." Sebastian followed Captain Hart around the outer rim of the large bowl that caused the dead water to pool. The light from the captain's torch showed many openings in the large cavern.

Shawndra helped Lady Jeanine sit on the cold rock and asked, "What are all these tunnels off of the cavern for?"

"They are choices," said Jeanine. For anyone who rightfully drinks the living water and becomes an Elder, their path becomes clear. They return to the people and help guide them in times of need. They become a voice of clarity. However, if anyone is rejected by the water, the last thing they want to do is return in disgrace. They may choose other paths. Some lead to death, some lead you deep into the mountain, some don't lead anywhere at all. But none of them will lead you back to the river.

Shawndra asked, "But the skeleton we saw on the path. The one you say had to be Aswan. Could she have drank from the source and made it back that far?"

Lady Jeanine replied, "I'm not convinced she ever made it this far."

"What do you mean, my lady? It's the only way to explain why she didn't have her standard with her," said Shawndra.

"We can figure that out later," said Lady Jeanine. "As soon as Captain Hart and Sebastian see that it's safe to go to the spring, we must go there quickly. My strength is fading, and I need to drink from the spring in order to replenish my life."

Sebastian was walking closely behind Captain Hart so that he could see from the light of the torch where to walk. As they neared the huddled mass on the rocks, they heard the water bubbling from the cave wall in front of them. Captain Hart kicked something that was metal and bent down to look at it. "What's this? It looks like a sword." He held the light close to it and picked it up.

Sebastian could see that it was indeed a sword. Hart used his cloak to clean off the grip, and Sebastian was surprised to see that the sword grip matched the carvings on his dagger that the bushy wild man gave him before they left Falls Lake.

"What does it mean?" asked Sebastian.

"I...I'm not sure," said Hart. He had a bewildered look on his face, as if he had been handed a piece that could make the whole puzzle make sense but he was struggling to find where it fit. "Sebastian, this was your father's sword. The dagger and the sword are a matching set, just like my dagger and sword." The oily figure in the spring moved again, and Hart turned quickly in that direction. Hart sheathed his sword and quickly ran to the sound of the spring where they had seen the huddled mass. Sebastian was close behind. Hart brought the torch close to the creature laying there. It was laying on its stomach facing the ground.

They could see now that it was a man, and he was wearing armor. A suit of armor with engravings that looked much like Hart's own armor. The man laying there had a damaged place on the plate that protected his back where it seemed someone stabbed him from behind. The wounded man gave a weak moan and seemed to try to move his arm but didn't have the strength. Hart grabbed the near lifeless man and rolled him over. One look at his face and Hart fell backwards, dropping the torch and almost knocking Sebastian over.

"It can't be...It's impossible!" gasped Captain Hart.

"Who is it?" called Lady Jeanine weakly.

"I'll tell you who it is," came a voice from the darkness. A gaunt form stepped out of one of the near by tunnels. Sebastian picked up the torch quickly and held it so that he could get a better look at this new figure. The man that stepped out of one of the tunnels looked more like a pale demon than a man. His garments were stained black and all of his body had a dim look about it. "He is Hart's mentor, former Captain of the Citadel, Cakal."

"How can this be? He disappeared thirteen years ago when he left to look for his brother," said Captain Hart.

"And he came here where he found me, Nabal!" screamed the creature from the darkness.

Sebastian took the torch and moved closer to his emaciated father lying in the stream that bubbled from the rock. He realized that the water that came from the opening of the rock was clean bright and sweet smelling. However, as it flowed over Cakal it turned black and had a stench and bubbled down into the pool as a thick oil. "Why is the water changing as it passes over this man? He must be the reason that the water has turned."

Sebastian began to drag his father from the water when Lady Jeanine spoke. "Sebastian, wait! You see, the water from the spring is the only thing keeping him alive."

"Yes boy, the water is keeping him alive. However, because he is lying in the spring, the water that runs over him is poisoned and so is all the land through which it flows. So which is it? Heal the land and kill the man, or save the man and kill the land?" An oily half smile could be seen spreading across Nabal's face, as if he was not telling them everything.

"Sebastian, we must think of our land before ourselves. We must take Cakal from the stream," said Captain Hart.

"Yes, take him. That would solve all of your problems, wouldn't it?" cried Nabal.

"I can't kill my own father," said Sebastian, as he cradled his father's head in his lap.

"Your father? You are the son of Cakal?" asked Nabal. It was the first time that he showed an expression that wasn't purely contempt or evil. "I was not aware that Cakal had a son. So, have you come to avenge your father's death?"

"He's not dead," said Sebastian. "He is still breathing."

"He may be living, but he's hardly alive. Look below him. The black death that poisons the land flows from him. Drag him from the stream, and you will save the land and end your father's misery," hissed Nabal.

"Sebastian, listen to wisdom," said Jeanine. "Nabal weaves lies into what he says. Learn the truth so that you do not act blindly."

"Then the land is doomed!" said Nabal.

"I'm sorry, Sebastian, I must do what is right for Crespin. Your father was my friend and my captain. But we must do what is right for all the people." There was a pained look on Captain Hart's face as he said this and placed his sword aside preparing to move Cakal from the spring.

"Wait!" cried Jeanine. She was growing weaker and could not even prop herself up without Shawndra's help. "You cannot remove him. He must stay in the stream. There is more to this than we know."

"Yes, let's listen to the old crone who could have made this journey at any time and saved young Sebastian's father. Let's listen to the keeper of secrets who speaks in riddles and never tells the truth." Nabal had stepped off the ledge and into the black pool of dead water and was wading across toward Lady Jeanine. "I remember your words. How you told me that only one who is worthy may drink from the spring. Only one that is called out by the living water may be an Elder. Well I came on the journey to the source of the spring, and I drank from it. It turned my heart black. I can no longer taste anything. I don't feel anything but contempt, and it's all your fault. You should have never told me about the spring in the first place."

Shawndra drew Lady Jeanine's sword and stood between her and Nabal. "Don't come any closer to her, or I'll chop off the closest thing to me."

"Child," said Nabal in a hushed tone, "I have no desire to harm the dear lady. Time will do that for me. You see that she is getting weaker now by the moment. Soon she will be dead, and the world will be rid of these annoying Elders." As he turned he kicked the pool so that the water splashed on Lady Jeanine, and she cried out as if she was in pain. Shawndra turned to her and went to her side and saw that the Lady was aging back to her old self. The body she had before they began their journey from Falls Lake.

"You see how weak she is; she can't even stand a little sprinkle." Nabal's laugh sounded more like a wheeze as he made his way to Sebastian and Captain Hart. "You see that I am unarmed, my good captain," said Nabal as he held his hands outstretched with palms facing out. "Do not harm an unarmed and innocent person. It's against your code."

"You are unarmed, and for that alone I will not strike you down. But you are far from innocent. What did you do to Cakal?" Asked Hart turning to Cakal who was laying in the stream with Sebastian cradling his head.

At that moment, Nabal pulled a small dagger from under his cloak and brought it down toward Hart's head. Hart saw him out of the corner of his eye and moved in time that the blade sank into an unprotected place beside his neck on his right side. The blade had been soaked in the dead water, and Hart fell to the ground and a coldness began spreading over the right side of his body. He could not move his arm and found himself unable to stand.

At that moment Sebastian jumped from his father and drew his dagger and slashed at Nabal. Nabal jumped backwards because he knew as long as he stayed in the dead pool then none of the group could follow him.

"What will you do now, boy?" screamed Nabal. "You can't defend both of these fools that have dropped their guards!"

"What do you mean both?" said Sebastian. And then he realized why his father had a stab wound on his back. "You are the one who attacked my father!" shouted Sebastian. "You are the one who placed him here, admit it."

"Of course I did, boy. What else could leave a stench so bad that could turn the land of the living water into a toxic swamp? What could be more revolting than a brother's betrayal?"

Sebastian stood defiant with his dagger in one hand and his other hand searching his knapsack for something else, anything else, he could use to defend himself. "What do you mean, a brother's betrayal?"

Nabal turned to Lady Jeanine and smiled. "You didn't tell him? Oh how delicious, you don't know that the shell of a man you call a father is also my brother. That's right, Sebastian, I am your uncle. Now won't you come over here and give your poor old uncle a hug." Nabal gave an evil grin and took a step toward Sebastian.

"Uncle or not, I'll not let you near me or my friends." Sebastian moved so that he was standing over his father. He could not find anything in his knapsack he could use to defend himself, but he saw his father's sword near and he quickly switched the dagger to his left hand and picked up the sword of Cakal with his right.

"So this is how it is. A little girl will defend the Elder Jeanine and a little boy will defend the two captains. Stabbing my brother in the back turned the pool to poison. I wonder what will happen when I dispatch the rest of you and leave your bodies to rot in this pool? I wonder how the land of Crespin will suffer then?" said Nabal with a growl.

Just then someone could be heard climbing the rocks to the top of the pool. The rustle of armor could be heard and then Ba'ar swung himself up to the rim of the pool. "Ba'ar, am I glad to see you," said Sebastian. "This is the man that is responsible for poisoning the waters of the Jezreel River and for attacking Captain Hart and the rest of us. He wants to kill us all and destroy what's left of Crespin. Now Nabal, you will be defeated."

Ba'ar stood in place and did not draw his weapon. He looked at the surroundings and his eyes settled on Captain Hart.

"What are you waiting for, Ba'ar, draw your sword and help us," said Shawndra.

"Don't bark your orders at me, girl," said Ba'ar. "I am a soldier and you are a child and it's time you learned your place." In that moment, Ba'ar drew his sword and with a powerful swing struck the sword Shawndra was holding and it flew into the dead pool and disappeared underneath the blackness.

"What are you doing?" cried Sebastian. "We can beat Nabal and heal the land."

"Why would I want to help you?" said Ba'ar. "It's because of you that I'm disgraced for trying to save my own life in Sodorrah. It's because of you that I can't go home to the Citadel. So, why should I help you?"

"Hear me," hissed Nabal as he turned to Ba'ar. "Join with me and I'll see to it that you return as the hero of Crespin. Everyone will hear of how you saved Sodorrah and how your comrades all perished foolishly in the dead water in the cave of the spring.

"How can you guarantee this? Sodorrah is held by Bolo and many townspeople. How will you keep them and the Baruk silent?" asked Ba'ar who was now very interested in Nabal's proposition.

"There are more in these mountains than just me. People whose minds have been clouded by the dead water. I will lead them against Sodorrah and the Baruk, and we will not go past Falls Lake. You and I can rule all of Crespin. We will carve up the land between us. And no one will return to tell any stories other than how Ba'ar is the savior of Crespin."

Ba'ar envisioned himself no longer as a mere captain of the Citadel, but a king ruling from Crescent City. The people of the land would bow before him or be crushed. All he had to do was help this repulsive creature for a time. After a while, he could eventually get rid of Nabal, and he wouldn't share power with anyone.

"What must I do?" said Ba'ar.

"Ba'ar, what are you doing?" cried Sebastian. "You are betraying your people and your captain."

"My people will be better served with me as their king. And as for him, he marked me a coward, and for that he will die!" shouted Ba'ar.

"The first thing you must do is get rid of the Lady Jeanine. Throw her into the dead pool!"

Ba'ar moved toward the lady but Shawndra leaped at him to try to stop him. Ba'ar swatted her aside, and she fell against the rocks and was knocked unconscious. Ba'ar then picked up Jeanine and looked into her aged face. "Not even an Elder can stand in my way now." Then Ba'ar hurled the last of the Elders into the dead pool and saw her grey hair disappear as it sank below the thick oily water.

"No," Sebastian cried out as he stretched his hand out across the dead water in vaine.

"Now we move together and finish off this whelp and his captain and leave their bodies to rot," said Nabal.

"Very well," said Ba'ar as he and Nabal moved to attack Sebastian from two different directions. Ba'ar moved around the edge, avoiding the dead water while Nabal waded through it to attack from Sebastian's left. Sebastian knew he couldn't defend from two directions, but he also knew he could not leave his father or Captain Hart. Captain Hart had propped himself against the rock ledge and was pale from the poisonous water running through his veins. He could barely whisper, "Run, Sebastian, go get help."

Sebastian stood over his father as tears began to stream down his face, "I will not leave my father or my captain. If I have to die here, then so be it. I will die with honor. But both of you will live on in disgrace."

Ba'ar's eyes narrowed as he said, "How dare you lecture me. I am a soldier of the Citadel, and I will make you pay for that."

As Sebastian held his father's sword and dagger, he trembled, knowing that at any moment both Ba'ar and Nabal would rush at him and his life would be over. He could not stop his tears from flowing and rolling down his cheeks. They puddled up on his chin and one single drop fell. It fell onto his father's skin, and in that moment Cakal gasped for breath.

It startled Sebastian, but it startled Nabal even more. This was the first sign of life that Cakal had given in thirteen years. As his breath became less labored, the water that flowed from around him began to clear and the black poisonous liquid that had previously flowed from him ceased. The water that flowed around him was alive again.

Nabal watched as the water in the pool began to clear and a light began to come from the pool. Nabal screamed and rushed to the edge of the pool before the living water could reach him. He threw himself onto the edge, but some of the water had made it onto his skin and he cried out. "What has happened? What have you done?"

Ba'ar was confused by all of this and saw how the water was now alive and flowing over the edge of the pool and the stench of the cave was being replaced by the sweet aroma of the spring. Sebastian was still standing over his father and looking down to him. His father opened his eyes and looked to Sebastian and they both smiled.

"What is going on here, Nabal? What is happening?" cried Ba'ar.

"Cakal, my brother, is healed. The water is living again. Quickly, kill the boy and throw him into the pool. That is our only hope." Ba'ar rushed forward and with a maneuver of his sword disarmed

Sebastian. Sebastian fell into the pool and tried to get away, but Ba'ar was too quick and too strong and was soon standing over him.

"Only a foolish boy!" said Ba'ar in a low hiss as he raised his sword to strike him a fatal blow. At that moment, the water erupted with a huge splash, and Ba'ar's sword was broken at the hilt. He spun around and standing before him was the Lady Jeanine in all her youthful beauty holding her own sword.

"Are you ready to do battle with an Elder, boy?" Ba'ar's face could not hide the fear that he had as he scrambled toward the edge of the pool but was kicked from behind and landed on the rocky ledge.

Nabal, seeing that he could not win, scrambled to a nearby cave and ran into the dark.

"I'm unarmed!" screamed Ba'ar. "You can't kill an unarmed man." Ba'ar began to cry and whimpered, "Please don't kill me."

Lady Jeanine leaned close, "I'm not going to kill you, Ba'ar. But one day she might." Lady Jeanine pointed to Shawndra who was pulling herself to her feet with a confused look on her face. "No Ba'ar, your days are not over, but if you return to this cave, I will see to it that the remainder of your days are full of pain." Jeanine raised up and placed her sword at Ba'ar's neck. "Now go and join Nabal, wherever that coward has run off to."

Ba'ar climbed out of the pool and ran along the edge. As he passed Shawndra, she kicked him in the knee which caused him to trip and fall over the edge of the pool, and they could hear the thuds and clanks as he fell to the bottom of the rough steps.

"I just wish I had an axe instead of a boot," said Shawndra as she rubbed her bruised shoulder and head. "My lady, you are well again?"

"Yes Shawndra, I feel better than I have in many years." Lady Jeanine waded over to Sebastian and held out her hand to help him up. As Sebastian and Lady Jeanine climbed out of the pool, Lady Jeanine knelt next to Captain Hart and squeezed the water from her sleeve over the wound on his neck. Instantly the wound was healed, and the Captain regained his strength. Sebastian and Lady Jeanine then pulled Cakal from the water and helped him to sit up.

Cakal said, "I feel as though I have just awoke from a terrible nightmare."

Lady Jeanine replied, "In many ways that is exactly what you have done." She then motioned to Sebastian and said, "Cakal, this is the son you have never met. This is Sebastian."

"How could this be? I just left Falls Lake a short time ago," said Cakal. He turned to Sebastian and said, "This boy is more than ten years old."

"Thirteen years, to be exact," said the Elder. "You have been gone for thirteen years."

Cakal looked at Sebastian with wonder and then held him close. "You must be my son, you have the look of your mother." Cakal and Sebastian embraced each other for the first time. They both cried as Cakal said he was sorry for being away for so long.

Sebastian wiped the tears from his eyes and gave the Elder a puzzled look. "I understand that a brother's betrayal is what poisoned the dead water, but what healed it?"

Lady Jeanine smiled and said, "That is why you are so important, Sebastian. The only thing that can overcome the stench of a brother's betrayal is the power of a son's loyalty and love. You were willing to defend your father to the death. The moment that the courage of your tears touched your father, the curse of Nabal's treachery was reversed. So you see, only you could bring about the healing necessary for the land and for your father."

"My goodness. You did all that for me, and you've never even met me," said Cakal. He looked as though he was about to burst with pride. "You are my son. Now, help me up from here."

Sebastian and Captain Hart picked up Cakal, and Hart began filling him in on what had happened in Crespin over the last thirteen years. As they spoke, the living water poured out of the giant stone bowl and cascaded down and out of the cave. The oily film created by the dead water was melting away and the light of the cave began to shine.

Suddenly, from the crack in the stone wall where the living water flowed from, a giant burst of water came out. A shimmering fountain flowed from the wall and all the water shone with a new life and brilliance, and in the midst of the spectacular display a large shape began to form. Lady Jeanine fell to the ground face first as a giant figure made up entirely of living water formed at the center of the pool and walked toward the group. The water seemed to flow wildly in the form of a person with a giant crown on its head, and a voice that was the same one from Sebastian's dream the night before could be heard.

"I am the Great Mai, king under the mountain."

Shawndra's mouth gaped open, and she and Sebastian froze in place. Cakal and Hart both bowed low as the figure spoke. "I am the one who called the Elders to my service. I am the one who blessed Crespin with the living water. And I am the one who has spared the life of Cakal these thirteen years."

Lady Jeanine raised her head and said, "I am Jeanine, your servant. What would you have us do, my king?"

Mai continued. "I have come to speak with the boy named Sebastian. Step forward." Sebastian was already on the narrow stone ledge that surrounded the pool. He hesitated and then took a step forward, off the path and onto the water itself. He was amazed that he was now standing on top of the water.

Mai spoke, "I have known you and set you apart since you were born. Hear my words and heed my wisdom. If you will follow my teachings and walk in my guidance, I will make you a king one day. Your name shall be the highest among men. But hear me well, if you turn from me, then I will uproot your line and cast it into the Valley of Dry Bones."

Sebastian was speechless at this proclamation.

Mai continued, "Give me the sword of your father."

Sebastian looked around and found the sword where it had landed when Ba'ar had knocked it out of his hand. He held it out, hilt first, to Mai and the glistening arm took it and living water covered it. Immediately the rust and tarnish left it, and it was shimmering and made new again. Mai handed it back and said, "You will train as a soldier and gain wisdom. You shall gain favor in the sight of men, as well as the sight of Mai."

Upon finishing these words, the water from the wall returned to a spring and the form of Mai disappeared. Sebastian was left to ponder these things and said, "I had so many questions to ask him. Where did he go?"

Jeanine replied, "He said all he wished to say. He went where he wished to go. You must remember that the Great Mai is not a calm wanderer. He is a powerful and wild king. He has chosen to bless you. Now you must honor that blessing.

Captain Hart stood up and said, "And I will make sure you do just that. Sebastian, I am making you my personal squire. I will teach you all you need to know about soldiering."

Cakal reached his hand over and placed it on Sebastian's shoulder, "I'm proud of you, my boy. You will make a fine squire."

"What about me?" asked Shawndra. "I came on this journey as well. What do I get?"

Lady Jeanine smiled and said, "I don't think there

are any rules about a knight having two squires, do you, Captain?"

Captain Hart looked at Shawndra and scratched his chin, "No, there are no rules against it, but there has never been a girl in the Citadel. But then again, a lot of things have happened today for the first time. Very well, Shawndra, I will teach you as well. You will be a squire. But you'll have to do everything the others do."

Shawndra said with a smile, "I wouldn't have it any other way."

Cakal interrupted, "I hate to break up the celebration, but since I haven't used my legs for thirteen years, I don't know how I'm going to make it out of here. You can't carry me all the way to Falls Lake."

"I can carry him," came a new voice from bottom of the cave.

Everyone walked to the edge and didn't see anyone. All they saw was Balam, the horse.

Sebastian said, "Since Balam doesn't have to stay out of the water anymore, he walked right in through the cave. But whose voice did we hear?"

"It was mine, silly," said the strange voice again.

Sebastian almost tumbled off the stone stairs when he realized that it was the horse that was speaking. "Did any of you hear that? Balam is speaking!"

"Of course I'm speaking," said the horse. "I've always been speaking. I guess you humans have finally settled down enough to listen."

Lady Jeanine skillfully descended the steps to stand

before Balam. "It's more than that, I suspect. Tell me, horse, did you drink any of the living water?"

"I haven't seen or smelled water like this ever. It was so sweet I had to drink. Am I in trouble?" The horse looked at Sebastian. "You're all looking at me the way Farmer Levert looks at me when I'm in trouble."

Sebastian said, "So, if the dead water would dull his mind and make him crazy, the living water makes him smarter and able to speak."

Lady Jeanine replied, "That's right. The horse is now like the Baruk. Not all creatures will have the same reaction to the water, but one thing is sure, things will be different now in Crespin."

Captain Hart and Shawndra were helping Cakal down the rocky steps when Shawndra said, "So, the Baruk will be well again, the people, as well as the land, will be healed, and people will be able to live in Falls Lake again. That sounds like a happy ending."

Lady Jeanine raised and eye brow and said, "Not quite."

"What do you mean, not quite?" asked Shawndra.

Sebastian looked to the ceiling and spoke, "What she means is that even though the living water flows, thirteen years of dead water will not be erased so quickly."

"That's right, Sebastian," said the Elder. We have new allies as well as new enemies. Your uncle is still out there, and now he has a friend in Ba'ar."

Captain Hart helped Cakal onto Balam's back and

said, "We haven't seen the last of Ba'ar. And there are plenty of mad people from Sodorrah that escaped into the mountains before we took control."

Sebastian scratched his head and said, "So, this really is a new beginning."

Lady Jeanine smiled at him and said, "Always remember you are not alone."

Shawndra punched Sebastian in the arm and said, "I'll be at the Citadel with you to watch your back and to make sure you don't get too soft."

Balam spoke up, "And I'll be around to carry you wherever you need to go."

Cakal said, "It looks like you've got everything well in hand, son. Let's get going, and you can fill me in on the last thirteen years that I've missed."

Map of
Crespin

Cave
of the
Source

Sunereek

Falls
Lake

Baruk   Land

Cities
of
Refuge

Citadel

Podo People

Valley of
the Beasts

Crescent
City

Agri   Plains

Agri   Plains

Jarrad   River

Agri Plains

Acadia

Acadian Shoals

N

PROLOGUE

And so it was that the young shepherd boy became a squire, a father was saved by his son, and the land was healed from the dead water. But as the Elder said, this was just the beginning. The Great Mai had set Sebastian on a path that would test his courage and loyalty. Sebastian would have peace for a season until he would again be called to face the darkness that resides in the hearts of men. He would journey to Crescent City and make new allies and face old enemies. So, prepare yourself to hear of our future king's adventures in *Sebastian Squire and the Crescent Coliseum*.

Coming Soon:

Sebastian Squire and the Crescent Coliseum
(Book two of five in the Sebastian Series)